W9-AHA-555

What the critics are saying...

๛

"TRACE'S PSYCHIC is a fast-paced paranormal romance. The suspense and drama keep you on the edge of your seat...TRACE'S PSYCHIC is a must read for those who love their sex peppered with the paranormal." ~ *The Road to Romance*

"Trace's Psychic is an action-packed paranormal romance that is scorching in its erotic intensity... The mystery surrounding the dying psychics is scary and intense. It will have you on the edge of your seat. Ms. Strong pens a fantastic tale of lust and fear... You won't want to miss this story!" ~ *A Romance Review*

"Trace's Psychic was just an awesome read for me. It hit on all the great points that make a wonderful story...Anyone that loves a good Psychic, mystery and sexy love story go and buy Trace's Psychic." ~ *Enchanted In Romance*

"I love paranormal books and this one is certainly worth the time...This couple is perfect together and the love scenes are totally hot, so keep some ice handy. This is the first book at Ellora's Cave for Jory Strong and she is off to a great start. I will certainly be looking for her books in the future." ~ *The Romance Studio*

"TRACE'S PSYCHIC by Jory Strong is a unique and powerful tale filled with passion, magic, action and adventure. I was truly mesmerized by Trace and Aislinn…This novel is extremely erotic and definitely not for the faint of heart. I highly recommend this read for anyone who is the mood for a great sexual journey." ~ *Romance Junkies*

Jory Strong

Trace's Psychic
Supernatural Bonds

ELLORA'S CAVE
ROMANTICA PUBLISHING

An Ellora's Cave Romantica Publication

www.ellorascave.com

Supernatural Bounds: Trace's Psychic

ISBN 1419952129
ALL RIGHTS RESERVED.
Supernatural Bounds: Trace's Psychic Copyright © 2004 Jory Strong
Edited by Sue-Ellen Gower
Cover art by Syneca

Electronic book Publication January 2005
Trade paperback Publication June 2005

With the exception of quotes used in reviews, this book may not be reproduced or used in whole or in part by any means existing without written permission from the publisher, Ellora's Cave Publishing, Inc.® 1056 Home Avenue, Akron OH 44310-3502.

This book is a work of fiction and any resemblance to persons, living or dead, or places, events or locales is purely coincidental. The characters are productions of the authors' imagination and used fictitiously.

Content Advisory:

S – ENSUOUS
E – ROTIC
X - TREME

Ellora's Cave Publishing offers three levels of Romantica™ reading entertainment: S (S-ensuous), E (E-rotic), and X (X-treme).

The following material contains graphic sexual content meant for mature readers. This story has been rated E–rotic.

S-*ensuous* love scenes are explicit and leave nothing to the imagination.

E-*rotic* love scenes are explicit, leave nothing to the imagination, and are high in volume per the overall word count. E-rated titles might contain material that some readers find objectionable—in other words, almost anything goes, sexually. E-rated titles are the most graphic titles we carry in terms of both sexual language and descriptiveness in these works of literature.

X-*treme* titles differ from E-rated titles only in plot premise and storyline execution. Stories designated with the letter X tend to contain difficult or controversial subject matter not for the faint of heart.

Also by Jory Strong

About the Author

Jory has been writing since childhood and has never outgrown being a daydreamer. When she's not hunched over her computer, lost in the muse and conjuring up new heroes and heroines, she can usually be found reading, riding her horses, or hiking with her dogs.

Jory welcomes comments from readers. You can find her website and email address on her author bio page at www.ellorascave.com.

TRACE'S PSYCHIC
Supernatural Bonds

~

Trademarks Acknowledgement

ဢ

The author acknowledges the trademarked status and trademark owners of the following wordmarks mentioned in this work of fiction:

Associated Press: Associated Press, The

Bailey's: R & A Bailey & Co

Dos Equis: Cerveceria Moctezuma, S.A.

Kahlua: The Kahlua Company

Starbucks: Starbucks U.S. Brands

Tums (Fastchew Tums): SmithKline Beecham Corporation

Prologue

∞

The girl-child was uncharacteristically quiet. Where usually she was a dizzying whirl of laughter and motion, today she stood by her mother's side with the stillness of a delicate fey creature surrounded by condemning spirits.

Her mother had warned her not to speak unless spoken to, not to try and touch any of the beautiful animals that she might see, or the shiny gold statuettes, or the sparkling gems.

All these things belonged to the man they were going to visit—her *nonanti*, her grandfather—though she wasn't to call him that unless he gave her permission, and she wasn't to get her hopes up that he'd grant that permission.

Why this was the case, the girl-child didn't understand. She knew only that since coming to this place, her mother had changed.

Or maybe her mother had always been like this, but because the child rarely saw her, she hadn't understood before.

The child's lip quivered. She missed Moki.

Moki was a warm hug and big pockets always full of magical items. Moki was music and singing, stories of mysterious places and gypsies who traveled all over the country and had great adventures. Moki was the mother of her heart, the woman who'd taken care of her every day since her birth.

She missed Moki. She wanted to leave this place and go back home. But her true mother said that she must forget about Moki and concentrate on fitting in here.

"Bring the child forward," the man on the shining, gem-covered chair said. He did not smile, nor was his voice welcoming.

The girl-child tried to be brave, though it was hard. Her mother's hand tightened on her own and she thought her mother might be afraid of the man as they took the few steps necessary to reach the place where he sat.

"What do you call her?" the man asked.

"Aislinn."

"And what of her father?" The man's lips twisted with distaste. "The human?"

"He's dead. Along with the rest of his band members." There was a small, almost silent sob, before Aislinn's mother added, "Their tour bus went off the road during a storm."

The man turned his attention to the girl-child. "She has the look of one of us. Let me see her ears."

Aislinn's golden locks were pulled back to expose the delicate pointed ears. She twitched, wanting to cover them. It still felt awkward to go without the butterfly earrings that Moki had always insisted she wear during the day so that she wouldn't be ridiculed for having funny ears.

The man said nothing for several minutes. Then he said, "Half-elf, half-human. She may stay here until she is old enough to be tested. If she proves to have our powers, then she may live among us. If not, then she must be returned to the human world."

Chapter One

ஐ

"Son of a bitch, Trace, I hate this stuff!" Detective Dylan Archer said as he stomped into the homicide bullpen.

Trace Dilessio grimaced at the sight of the newspaper in his partner's hand. He'd seen it himself when he stopped for breakfast this morning. Fuck, he might as well have ordered cardboard for all the pleasure he got out of his meal.

He'd been up half the night doing what he could to help locate the missing Morrison kid and it wasn't even his case. Thank God.

He was a murder detective, not a Missing Persons cop. But he'd pitched in all the same because everybody on the force knew that the more time elapsed, the less likely things were going to end well.

Then the parents had rushed off to some psychic, and suddenly the kid was found.

It stunk like a publicity stunt.

And like pouring salt in a wound, this morning's article had suggested that the police should be more open-minded and consult the psychics on missing person's cases. The play it was getting on the TV was even worse.

Trace gritted his teeth just thinking about it. This psychic shit always managed to push his buttons.

"I say we have vice run a raid on this psychic operation," his partner said. "There's bound to be something we can bring them in on."

Trace shook his head. "Yeah, and the newspapers would have a field day with that, Dylan. Be grateful it's not our case. What goes around comes around. Eventually the psychic involved in this stunt will get what's coming to them. Now let's hit the road. We've got a full day ahead of us."

Dylan dropped the newspaper on his desk. "Hey, you're still on for after work, right?"

Trace shrugged. "Yeah, sure."

* * * * *

The chime sounded over the doorway and Aislinn looked up from where she was dusting the glass shelves and rearranging a display of crystals. It still made her nervous when Moki left her in charge of Inner Magick, but when she saw who'd come in, Aislinn relaxed. She counted Sophie as one of her truest friends.

"I won't take no for an answer," Sophie said, putting her hands on her hips and scowling for effect. The crystals dangling from her ears echoed the green fire in her eyes.

Aislinn laughed softly and held her hands in the air, acknowledging defeat. "I'll go, but only for a little while. I promised to be somewhere tonight."

Sophie frowned. "Tell me that you're not going over to that...person's...place tonight."

"He has some talent, and he's been kind to me."

Sophie snorted. "Of course he's been kind to you. He wants to screw you — literally and figuratively."

"It's not like that. Patrick is a friend. He's not interested in me in a sexual way." Aislinn ducked her head to hide a smile. She knew what Sophie's next words would be.

"Right. He'd jump you in a second, so would most of the guys who meet you. I mean, look at you. You're like something out of a fairy tale—tiny and beautiful." Sophie paused and looked down at her own tall, lithe figure, before adding, "Next to you, I'm an Amazon. I hate you."

Aislinn laughed. "You always say that, but whenever we go out together, by the end of the night you have the men begging for your phone number."

Sophie snorted again. "Only because they don't get anywhere with you. You know, just because ninety-nine-point-nine percent of the guys don't believe in anything besides beer and football doesn't mean that you can't enjoy having one of them in your life. At worst they won't say anything about this—" Sophie waved her hand toward the displays containing crystals, tarot cards and runes, "—and at best, once they see you've got talent and aren't some hokey fortune-telling-fake, then they'll actually be interested in what you do. But—and here's the big ugly but—you've got to actually date one of them! And to date one of them, you've got to first *meet* one of them. Which luckily for you, is where I come in."

Aislinn couldn't stop herself from smiling. "Are we meeting up with any of your friends tonight?"

"Tiffany and my cousin Storm. The cop. You've met her a couple of times. She's the one Moki did a reading for a while back. Speaking of Moki, it seems like she's been gone forever. When's she coming back?"

"I don't know. She said that traveling with her family again made her homesick for the old days. When I talked to her last night, they'd just gotten to Italy."

Aislinn moved one last crystal to form a new arrangement, then stood up. "I can leave now if you like."

Sophie huffed. "Tell me you're not going in that outfit."

Looking down at the jeans and oversized work shirt, Aislinn frowned. "What's wrong with this?"

"Nothing if you want someone to have to guess whether you have breasts or not." Sophie pointed toward the back of the store and the stairway that lead to the upstairs apartment. "Go! I'll lock up for you."

Aislinn laughed, but gave in and headed to her apartment. When it came to stubborn, she knew that she was no match for Sophie. And it was not as though she truly objected to dressing up, or that she had no breasts—she did, though they were in proportion to the rest of her, which meant small when compared to non-elfin women.

A hint of despair touched Aislinn. Not elfin. Half-elfin. A distinction that meant everything among her mother's people and to her mother, especially after she'd heartbonded with a high-caste Elf-lord.

Aislinn rubbed a finger over the silver and crystal butterfly earrings that perched at the top of her ears and cleverly concealed what no human was supposed to see. Plastic surgery wasn't an option. Even if she could truly bring herself to have that part of her heritage cut away, she'd found that human medicine was unpredictable when it came to her body.

With a sigh, she pulled her hand away from her ear and opened the closet door. As if on cue, Sophie yelled up the stairs, "Wear the pale blue fuck-me dress!"

Aislinn laughed, but reached for the sundress anyway. She could just imagine what Sophie would say if she knew how truly inexperienced she was with men.

* * * * *

As soon as Trace walked into Lily's Place and saw Miguel and Conner in a non-cop bar with expectant smiles on their faces, he knew he was in trouble. "Shit, Dylan, you've set me up!"

Dylan laughed. "You're a detective all right, can't pull anything over on you." His eyebrows moved up and down. "I hate to say this, Trace, but since you sent your last girlfriend packing, you've been cranky as hell, which is a sure sign that a guy who's used to getting some isn't getting any. Since I know it's not from lack of offers, I figured you just needed a new face. Then out of the blue, this opportunity came along to meet some women. I did the only thing a partner can do, I took it upon myself to make the ultimate sacrifice and accept on your behalf."

Trace laughed as he and Dylan joined the other detectives.

"Not here yet," Miguel Torres, the newest member of the department said.

Dylan grinned. "They'll be here. Just try not to scare them off doing your desperate puppy routine when you see the tantalizing Officer Storm O'Malley."

Conner chimed in, "Ah man, he's not going to try and hump her leg, is he? I hate to see a cop doing that. It doesn't look good for the rest of us."

Miguel picked up his bottle of Dos Equis. "I'd hump every inch of her. Just remember she's mine."

Dylan rolled his eyes. "In your dreams. Last time I had my ears out, the word was that Officer O'Malley turned you down flat." He nodded toward Trace. "But tonight you're in luck. If fact, we're all in luck. Tonight gentlemen, we're going to get to watch a pro at work. We're going to learn how it's done from the guy who has to keep nametags next to his box of condoms so he can remember who he's fucking."

Trace shook his head. Shit. What would these guys say if they knew the truth? That the reason he went through so many women was because his dick never got satisfied. Yeah, he came. Yeah, the women came — always. He made sure of that. But it was like scratching an itch that never went away. He'd even tried having a live-in girlfriend, thinking maybe that would take the edge off. Wrong.

He shifted in his seat, feeling the pent-up need starting to build. Between trying to get the live-in out of his house when he was home and all the OT he'd been putting in at work in order to give her incentive to move on, it had been a while since he'd been with a woman.

Goddamn! Maybe Dylan wasn't bullshitting. Maybe he had gotten cranky without even realizing it. Maybe this was just what he needed. A hard, fast fuck. No promises. No strings. No recriminations.

Trace's cock jerked to attention and seconded the motion when a tiny blonde walked in with three other women a few minutes later.

"Oh yeah," muttered Conner. "Jackpot. I'd take any one of those three and leave the well-stacked Officer Storm O'Malley for Miguel."

The female officer in question spotted the men and said something to the other women. All three turned to look, but Trace felt like there was a hot wire leading from the blonde straight to his dick. "Who is she?"

Dylan laughed. "Here we go, men, The Pro is locked on to a target! Which one do you want?"

Trace shifted in his seat and ignored the question. The last thing he needed was for the guys to think they heard him panting. He'd never live that one down. Christ, he couldn't remember a time since he was a teenager when his cock had felt like this—like it was going to explode just from looking and fantasizing. And right now his fantasies were kicking into overdrive and they all involved him having the little blonde any way he wanted her.

He almost groaned out loud when the women headed for a booth. Great. They were going to have to do the "let's pretend we're not here to hook up with someone" bullshit before they could get to the actual fucking.

"Carumba," Miguel muttered. "Nothing is simple with her."

Dylan laughed and clapped Miguel on the shoulder. "Yeah, I can see she's hot for you." He stood up. "I'll go and suggest they join us."

Conner snickered. "Ten bucks says it's going to take more firepower than you have to get them over here."

"You're on. Anyone else in?"

Trace said, "I'll back you."

Miguel grinned. "My money's with Conner."

Dylan stood up and swaggered over to the booth. Trace's attention never left the blonde's face. His gut tightened when she smiled at his partner and extended a small, graceful hand. He couldn't stop the low growl from escaping. Until he got his fill, there was only going to be one man riding her. The blonde was in for a disappointment if she thought she was leaving tonight with anyone but him.

His partner's attention turned to the redhead and Trace felt some of the tightness leave his chest. The blonde was talking to one of the other women, not focusing on Dylan.

"I'll be goddamned," Conner muttered as he reached for his wallet and extracted a ten-dollar bill.

Trace watched the women leave their booth. Anticipation streaked through him along with another round of cock-jerking lust. Jesus, he couldn't remember being so turned-on, so fast.

Up until now he'd always considered himself a regular meat and potatoes kind of guy, a red-blooded man who liked his women with big boobs, a nice ass, and legs that didn't stop. He was flexible when it came to hair color and the ability to hold an intelligent conversation. And since he was a big guy—in every way—his women were usually tall, like the redhead Dylan seemed to be making a play for.

Trace grimaced. The blonde that had his dick aching was a whole different type than what he usually went for, and he wasn't convinced she could even take all of him, much less take him in all the ways he wanted to put it to her.

But man, it was going to be fun trying.

Miguel practically catapulted out of his chair when the women reached their table. He was grinning like a fool. Conner snickered and rolled his eyes at Trace. Trace laughed softly, but they also stood, each snagging a chair from a nearby table and pulling it over.

Dylan said, "Ladies, in order of importance, my partner, Trace Dilessio, then Detective Conner Stern and then, the baby of the department, Conner's partner, Miguel Torres."

The women took their seats and Trace wondered what he'd done to deserve the torture his body was putting him through. The little blonde was across the table from him, too far away to accidentally touch, but close enough that the scent of her seemed to have filled his lungs.

Dylan indicated the redhead and introduced her as Sophie. The dark-haired one was Tiffany.

It was all Trace could do to take his eyes off the blonde long enough to acknowledge the other women. His chest was starting to get as tight as his balls and from the look on his partner's face, Dylan was clued in to the fact and drawing out the introductions just to make him sweat.

"You all know Officer Storm O'Malley," Dylan said, waiting for the other detectives to acknowledge her while shooting Trace a grin.

Trace gritted his teeth. *Oh yeah, partner, payback is going to be hell.*

Dylan's grin only got more pronounced. "And finally, this is Aislinn Windbourne."

Trace used the introduction as an excuse to stare even harder. Christ, she was exquisite. Every individual feature looked as though a sculptor had labored so that it was flawless and fit perfectly with the whole.

Her slightly husky "hi" was breeze-soft, her voice caressing as it flowed over his skin. All he could think about was covering her lips with his and tasting the words as they came out of her mouth.

Goddamn, he had it bad. And if he wasn't careful, every cop at the table was going to see it. That was the major drawback with hanging out with other detectives—observation was second nature to all of them.

Dylan said, "Gentlemen, I've promised these lovely ladies that we'd buy the drinks if they'd sit with us."

None of the men complained. "No problema," Miguel said and waved a waitress over. Within minutes the four women had their drinks.

Trace would have figured Aislinn for a wine drinker. Instead she'd ordered a specialty coffee drink loaded with Bailey's, Kahlua, a hint of something else and topped with whipped cream and a cherry.

Out of the corner of his eye he saw Conner focus his attention on the dark-haired Tiffany while Miguel was a starving puppy who wanted to make a meal out of Storm. Dylan had settled on the redhead—no surprise there. Trace glanced at the clock behind the bar and wondered how long it'd be before Aislinn would give him the come-on smile.

These kinds of setups usually played out in a certain predictable pattern because the women who came around to meet cops were already halfway to putting out. There was something about a badge, a gun, and a uniform that was irresistible, no matter what the cop wearing them looked like, or acted like. Trace had seen the scrawniest, no personality, wet-behind-the-ears cadet just out of the academy reel in a babe the first time he put his uniform on and went out in public. In fact, Trace had seen it happen so many times that he didn't even blink anymore. Of course, being a detective, especially a homicide cop, had an additional perk. He didn't have to wear the uniform in order to get the women.

Aislinn took a sip from the coffee mug, then darted the tip of a small pink tongue across her upper lip to remove a thin line of whipped cream. Trace almost doubled over as a wave of lust surged through his cock. His hand made an involuntary movement in the direction of his lap. Erotic fantasies of him holding himself as she wrapped her lips around him and sucked him off played out in his imagination.

Across the table, Aislinn stilled and dropped her eyes. A delicate blush spread across her face as though she was reading his mind.

It didn't take any great detective skills to see that she was going to need some smooth handling. He winced as a fresh batch of erotic images flashed through his mind.

Christ. If he didn't get her out of here soon, he was going to disgrace himself.

Trace was used to women opening the conversation, asking about his cases and cuddling up close to let him know they were available. He couldn't even remember the last time he'd had to get a woman talking. If anything, he usually had the opposite problem—shutting them up.

He cleared his throat while his brain cells scrambled around for something to say that wouldn't come across as an interrogation or manage to scare her off. But before he could think of something smooth, something that wouldn't tip the other guys off to just how hungry he was for Aislinn, a slow song started playing and people wandered out to the dance floor. Aislinn's eyes followed them. Sadness flickered across her face briefly and Trace's heart did a little dive thinking maybe she'd just gotten out of a relationship.

Fuck. What was wrong with him tonight? She was here, which meant she was available. Period. And if she was trying to get over heartbreak, then he was her man. A fast, hard fuck with no strings would fix her right up.

Storm said, "Hey, isn't that one of your father's songs?"

Aislinn half smiled. "Yes. One of his last ones."

Conner turned his attention from the delectable Tiffany. "Jessie Wolfe was your father?"

The name was vaguely familiar, but Trace couldn't place it. His tastes ran more to country. The ballad playing reminded him of old Jethro Tull stuff.

Aislinn leaned toward Conner and something tightened in Trace's gut at the way her eyes darkened as her attention focused on the other man. "Not many people remember him," she said.

Conner grinned. "He was amazing. I have all five of his CDs. Play 'em at least once a month when I need inspiration."

Miguel groaned. "I'm not sure that's a good thing. Musical talent is a genetic thing and you were born without."

The soft smile that Aislinn directed at Conner was like a kick in the gut to Trace. "What instrument do you play?" she asked.

The big cop actually flushed, but then he surprised the hell out of Trace by giving Aislinn a straight answer. "I do a little bit on the electric guitar, but mainly the flute, like your father."

Aislinn said, "There was a sixth CD. It was never released."

"Can I get a copy of it?" Conner asked, leaning so close to her that it was all Trace could do to keep himself from jerking them apart.

"Yes."

"Great. I'll come by and get it."

Uncertainty flickered across Aislinn's face, but she nodded and something snapped inside of Trace at the thought of Conner going by Aislinn's place. He stood up abruptly and put his hand on her arm, pulling her from the chair. "Let's dance."

Dylan snickered while Miguel had the nerve to laugh out loud. Both reactions rolled over Trace, barely noticed. Now that he was touching Aislinn, he was having trouble thinking at all. The invisible wire leading from her to his dick had just heated up another hundred degrees. His balls were already tight and his cock had leaked a few drops. He wasn't sure he was going to make it through the slow dance with her body pressed to his, but there was no way in hell that he wasn't going to use it as an excuse to rub against her.

Fuck.

Yeah. That's what he needed all right. Maybe one dance would be enough of an intro and he could haul her out to the car and do her there, or better yet, on the beach. It wasn't his usual style, but desperate times require desperate means. His house was half an hour away and he'd be damned if he was going to go looking for a hotel room. She'd be way too skittish for that.

He pulled her onto the dance floor and into his arms, making sure that every possible inch of their bodies touched. They both tensed as soon as his erection was pressed against her soft abdomen. Trace tightened his grip around her and tried to keep from groaning at the exquisite sensation. Christ, this was incredible. He must have gone without too long. It had never been this intense before.

Trace closed his eyes and buried his face in her hair. The smell of her was just as intoxicating as the feel of her. As he stroked her back, she relaxed into him and cuddled his rock-hard cock. "Yeah, feel what you do to me," he whispered as he nuzzled her ear.

She lifted her face and masculine satisfaction whipped through him at her passion-drugged expression. She'd go with him all right, and she'd be responsive when he rode her. He pulled her up against him even tighter and brought his lips down so that they hovered just above hers.

Aislinn's heart fluttered wildly in her chest. Her body felt as though it belonged to someone else tonight — to him. It had from the moment she'd felt his gaze on her.

He was human and yet he beguiled her. Among her mother's people such a reaction usually meant that a couple was destined to bond. Her heart opened and hope rushed in like a giant hand that might just as easily crush her as stroke her.

She knew that here among her father's people things were different in ways that she didn't always understand. But even knowing that, Aislinn knew that she wouldn't be able to deny him. He called to her in a way that she couldn't refuse.

A low growl sounded in Trace's throat before he closed the distance and touched his lips to hers. She whimpered against his mouth and pressed more tightly against him. When his tongue pushed its way into her mouth and tangled with hers, she wanted to cry from the intimacy of it.

While she'd lived with her mother, no one had ever cuddled or held her, not even in friendship. She'd been an outcast for so many years, separated by her impure blood. It had left her vulnerable and cautious. That caution had followed her when she was cast from Elven-space.

Until now, she had not wanted to risk herself with any of the men she'd met. Trace's nearness, his warmth and heated embrace were a battering ram against her fragile defenses. Aislinn moved her tongue against his, following his lead as her body prepared itself for him.

The music faded into a fast song. Trace kept her close for several long seconds before ending the kiss and guiding her from the dance floor and out of the building.

She shivered despite the warmth of the night air. Her heart thundered in her ears and her steps slowed. He turned and cupped her face, then covered her lips again with his.

This kiss was more demanding than the one on the dance floor. His tongue stroked in and out of her mouth in a wet promise of what his cock was going to do to her. Aislinn whimpered and his hands moved down to her hips and pulled her tight against his erection. She was swollen and wet and needy, dazed by the desire flooding her system.

He pulled away and took her arm, guiding her to a car, only to get a blanket out of the trunk before leading her down the concrete stairs and onto the moonlit beach.

They passed several other couples, all lying on blankets, bare skin visible. Nervousness started to settle over Aislinn. Trace felt the change in her and stopped. Fuck, she was a skittish one. His cock was about to explode. There was no way in hell that he was taking her back before he got some relief.

"It's okay, baby," he whispered against her lips before plunging his tongue into her mouth. She immediately whimpered and yielded to him. Christ, she was so responsive, so submissive. It was driving him crazy. Until now he'd thought he just liked wild, rough sex, with a little bondage thrown in sometimes, but this...this was something else altogether, something he didn't have time to think too much about right now. If his cock and balls got any tighter, he was the one who would be on his knees begging.

He dropped the blanket then stroked up her leg. She shivered against him, but didn't protest when his hand slipped under her dress and along the wet crease of her panties. It was the last straw for him. If he didn't get inside her he was going to end up coming in his pants.

"Baby, I can't wait any longer," he whispered as his hands eased back up, taking her dress with them. He dropped the dress to the sand, almost panting at the sight of her standing there in her pale blue bikinis and see-through bra.

Her eyes were lust-dark with a hint of nervousness in them. Trace thought his cock might just jump out of his pants. He unzipped his jeans and took himself in hand. "Take your bra off," he demanded. Aislinn's small pink tongue darted across her lip and he had to squeeze himself to keep from being done right then and there.

She slid trembling fingers to the front of her bra and opened it. Trace groaned at the sight of pale pink nipples crowning perfectly formed breasts.

"Now the rest of it," he demanded, his voice barely recognizable.

She licked her lip nervously again. As she complied, more pre-cum coated the head of his cock. It was ecstasy. It was torture. He wanted to lick and kiss and bite every inch of her, to bury his face in her pussy and suck on her clit until she screamed. But his cock was making its own demands and Trace knew he'd have to put off exploring her body until later. He stopped long enough to spread the blanket out and strip his clothes off, then he was on her, pushing her to the blanket and covering her body with his.

Instinctively, Aislinn wrapped her arms and legs around Trace. He groaned and moved against her, running his rigid cock against her wet slit. She shivered, needing him, and yet a little afraid. He was so much bigger than she was, so much stronger.

His hands curled in her hair and pulled so that she had to meet his gaze. His face was flushed, his eyes were dark, and his mouth was pulled tight as though he were in pain. A foreign, primitive thrill shot through Aislinn at the sight of him, of what need for her was doing to him.

"Guide me into you," he ordered and she slid her hand down to where his massive erection rubbed against her swollen, wet nether lips.

Trace's breath strangled in his throat. Her soft hand almost finished him off. "Now," he demanded. If she so much as slid her fingers up and down his shaft he was going to come all over her.

Not that he wouldn't do that someday, but not today, not now. She whimpered again as she brought the tip of him to her entrance. The feel of her wet labia against the head of his penis brought a moment of sanity. "Fuck. I need a condom."

"It's safe," she whispered, tightening her legs around his waist.

His hips bucked against her and his cock slipped inside just enough to make Trace almost plead for death. She was so tight that it sent exquisite pain right up his shaft. "Oh baby, you're killing me," he panted as he reached down to cover her hand with his.

He worked himself in another inch, then pulled back, only to repeat the process over and over again. Her whimpers fed his hunger to the point that he couldn't control himself. The urge to pound into her, to dominate her with his body whipped through him in an unstoppable need.

Trace pulled her hand away from his cock and lifted it above her head then grabbed the other one and held it, too. Her eyes were fevered, wild, her face lifting to his, her lips begging for his. He covered her mouth and took her cries into himself as he slammed into her so hard and deep that he hit her cervix with every stroke. She screamed into his mouth and thrashed. Her back bowed in orgasm and her already tight channel gripped his cock so fiercely that Trace almost screamed himself. Fire raced down his spine and across his taut buttocks before rolling through his balls and shooting down the length of his cock as he came in an endless stream of pleasure so extreme that he knew he'd do anything to experience it again.

He didn't have the strength to pull out of her when he was finished. He only barely had enough strength left to hold his weight off of her long enough so that he could position them on their sides.

Aislinn's face was buried in his neck. Her body was shaking. Trace smoothed his hand along her back and buttocks until the shivering eased. "You okay, baby?" he whispered against her hair. When she nodded, he tightened his grip around her and kept her face in his neck. Christ, he ought to be asking if *he* was okay. Sex had *never* been like that before. And he was still inside her— without a condom.

Shit. He *never* took a woman without a condom. *Never*. Even if they swore they were on the Pill. His trust didn't go that far and an unplanned marriage because of an unplanned kid was *not* going to be part of his future.

More shaken than he was willing to admit, Trace eased out of Aislinn, only to have every muscle in his body tighten when he saw the small traces of blood on the inside of her thighs. Like a visceral memory, pleasure so exquisite it bordered on pain ripped through his cock and up his spine as he remembered how tiny her channel had been. He had to close his eyes against the need to put her on her hands and knees and mount her. Christ! What was wrong with him?

"Tell me you weren't a virgin," he said, flinching inwardly at the harshness of his own voice.

Aislinn's heart raced. She moved away from him and reached for her clothing. He grabbed her arm and pulled her against him, forcing her to look at him with his free hand.

"Tell me," he demanded again.

"It's okay," she whispered. "I wanted this."

"Fuck. Are you even on the Pill?"

Relief washed through Aislinn as the cause of his anger became clearer. One of the few things that her mother had prepared her for was this. There could be no pregnancy until there was a bond. "I'm protected," she told him, not wanting to lie yet not able to tell him the complete truth.

Trace stared at her for another tense moment, as a cop willing a suspect to confess and not as a lover. Some of the walls Aislinn had used to protect herself slid back into place, though the hope remained locked inside her heart. He let her go and reached for his clothes. Aislinn dressed quickly, flushing with embarrassment as she had to use the blanket to clean herself before slipping on her panties.

When they got back to the bar, Trace shot his partner a silent command to move so that he could put Aislinn next to him. Dylan grinned and moved over.

Sophie sent her a worried look and leaned close so that she could whisper, "Let's go to the ladies' room. Okay?" Aislinn nodded and followed her.

Before the ladies' room door could even close, Sophie grabbed Aislinn. "Tell me you didn't do what I think you did!"

Some of Aislinn's natural good humor returned in Sophie's comforting presence. "You told me to wear the pale blue fuck-me dress," she teased, then laughed out loud at the stunned expression on Sophie's face. Over the past several months Aislinn had learned that it took *a lot* to shock Sophie.

Sophie closed her eyes and groaned. When she opened them there was still concern on her face, but also a trace of humor. "Are you okay? I mean, he's not exactly what I had in mind. I thought Storm was going to fix us up with some regular guys, not these macho murder cops."

"I'm okay."

Sophie's brows drew together as she studied Aislinn. "You look okay on the outside." She bit her lip. "Look, I'd feel terrible if you got hurt. Don't get serious about him, okay? When the two of you left, Storm told me that she was hoping you and Dylan or you and Conner would hit it off. Trace is a player. He's got a revolving door on his bedroom."

Aislinn gave Sophie a hug as more of the walls around her heart slid into place and some of the hope faded. Her father's world might prove to be just as painful as her mother's world. "I'm okay," she repeated.

Sophie hugged her back. "So does this mean you're going to forget about going to Patrick's place tonight?"

Aislinn shook her head. "I promised that I would help him."

Sophie grimaced but spared Aislinn from her usual tirade on the subject of Patrick Dean.

When they got back to the table Aislinn risked a quick look at Trace's face. Her chest tightened painfully when she could find no warmth in his features, no softness. Only the tenderness between her thighs and the faint smell of him on her skin gave testament to the fact that they'd been intimate.

Sophie's warning rang in her ears and Aislinn steeled herself against disappointment by telling herself that whatever happened next, she was glad to have finally experienced what so many others took for granted.

Tiffany and Conner returned from the dance floor and took their seats. "I'm really impressed that you guys would all pitch in on a missing child case," Tiffany said as she reached for her beer.

Conner laughed and said, "I wouldn't mention it right now, it's still a touchy subject with Dylan and Trace. They pulled all-nighters in addition to working their own shifts."

Sophie took up the conversation. "Why's it a touchy subject? The kid was found, right? Don't tell me you guys are so territorial that you care which department found him."

Miguel rolled his eyes and pointed the neck of his beer bottle toward the other detectives. "The old-timers can be pretty territorial, but what's got them crazed is the psychic angle and the fact that it was probably a hoax."

Tiffany frowned. "What psychic angle?"

Miguel grinned. "I'd go get you a copy of this morning's paper, but I might get a bullet in the back, so I'll summarize—briefly. While we were busting our asses trying to find the kid, the parents supposedly went to see a psychic who mumbled some babble over a crystal ball and told them where the kid was and just like that, the kid is found, and the police department gets a black eye, or two. Now the newspapers and TV stations are on a jag, trying to get us to start consulting some nutcase psychic every time someone goes missing. And that's just for starters."

"Oh," Tiffany said in a subdued voice as she shot a look toward Sophie and Aislinn.

"Christ, I hate that psychic bullshit," Trace said. "I'd like to lock every single one of them up. They're all either con artists or whackos."

Dylan touched his beer bottle to Trace's. "I'm with you partner."

For a second Aislinn couldn't think. The blood roared in her ears as though it was rushing from her heart and leaving behind a huge, gaping hole. Sophie's hand on her arm brought a measure of calm, and with it, thought. She needed to leave. There was nothing for her here. There would never be anything for her here. She cherished the psychic gifts that she'd inherited along with her elfin blood. Without them she had nothing to offer, no way to fit into this human world.

On legs that trembled slightly, Aislinn stood. "It's been nice meeting you, thank you for the drink."

Trace started to rise from his chair saying, "I'll walk you to your car." But before he'd even finished the sentence Aislinn was shaking her head no and holding her hand up as if to ward him off. "That's okay. I've got to run." And she did just that, whirling and escaping the bar before he could even clear his chair.

Trace stood there staring at where she'd been. He felt like he'd taken a head shot. What had just happened?

Yeah, he was still reeling from the fact that she'd been a virgin. Yeah, he was still feeling a little stressed by the whole unprotected sex thing, even though she'd said she wouldn't get pregnant. It wasn't in his nature to trust. And it sure as hell wasn't in his nature to lose control like that and go in without taking care of the protection himself.

But Christ, that didn't mean he wanted to quit after only one fuck. Hell no. There was no way his cock was going to go for that. He'd only come back into the bar in order to get himself back under control...and to give her tight little channel a break before he took her home and rammed himself back into her until neither of them could move.

So what the fuck had just happened? And why did he want to howl like a kid whose favorite of all favorite possessions had just been taken away?

Chapter Two

ဆ

Aislinn was ashamed of the tears that streaked down her face as she drove. She dashed them away with the back of her hand and drew a shaky breath. She was stronger than this, she'd had to be in order to survive Elven-space.

She needed to stop crying, now, before she got to Patrick's house. If he saw that she was upset, he'd try to use it as an excuse to comfort her. Despite what she'd told Sophie, Aislinn knew that Patrick's interest in her included a desire for sex.

But she also knew that it wasn't *her* he was attracted to so much as her ability to coax magic from crystals and to find missing people — humans — though he didn't know there was a distinction. Both were meager talents when compared to what a true elf could do, but among her father's people they allowed Aislinn to contribute, to be part of a greater whole.

She took another deep breath, this one less shaky than the last one. Everything would be okay. She needed to put what happened with Trace into perspective, to look at it like Sophie would look at it.

Hadn't Sophie confused love and lust a few times and cried on Aislinn's shoulder afterward? Thinking about those times eased the terrible knot in Aislinn's chest somewhat.

Even among the Elven, it wasn't uncommon for men and women to have an assortment of partners before finally settling into a heartbond. Surely there was sometimes a confusion as to which feelings sprang from the soul and which came from the body. Perhaps it was the human side that had confused lust with the beguilement that happens among those destined to bond.

Aislinn rubbed a hand over her heart and willed the last of the hope to leave its depths. She would be more careful next time, more cautious. And if she decided to share herself with someone again, she'd be better prepared so that it wouldn't end with tense questions and chilly silence.

Feeling more like herself, she pulled into Patrick's driveway and frowned at the lack of light coming from the house. The tips of her ears tingled as the crystals in her butterfly earrings transmitted a muted warning to her. It didn't help that Patrick's driveway was so overgrown by shrubs that even the moonlight had a difficult time getting through the thick foliage.

She ran a finger along the delicate wings on one of the butterfly earrings and chewed on her bottom lip, wondering if the uneasiness slithering along her backbone meant that Patrick was inside preparing to hold a séance for the mystery person he was seeing tonight. She'd already warned him that she wouldn't participate in trying to call spirits back from the dead.

Aislinn shivered, tempted to leave. But Patrick had pleaded with her, telling her that the person he was seeing tonight was the most important person he'd ever seen and she'd promised to be here, for moral support. Aislinn shivered again, but opened her door and got out of the car. Honor was everything to the elves, and even though her blood wasn't pure, she wouldn't stain her honor by failing to keep her word.

With each step down the darkened driveway, the sense of foreboding grew in Aislinn's chest. Twice she opened her mouth to call out, but each time some instinct held her back.

The front door to Patrick's house was unlocked and slightly open. Aislinn pushed forward into the hallway. The smell of incense was heavy and sweet. She flipped the light switch and only barely managed to contain her scream at the blood-coated scene in front of her.

* * * * *

One by one the women made their excuses and left the bar. "Well, that was a bust," Conner said as Tiffany's ass disappeared through the door.

Miguel looked deeply into his beer bottle and sang in a low, off-key voice, "So close and yet so far away," which netted him a whack on the back of the head from Conner.

Dylan grinned. "Hey, it wasn't a total bust. The Pro did his thing and got something that will hopefully make him a less grumpy partner, though I admit, it wasn't The Pro's usual style and it did seem to go a little sideways there at the end, but..." A couple of pagers hummed simultaneously at the table.

Trace was the first one to read his and get a cell phone out. As soon as the others heard him reach the station dispatcher, they paused, waiting to see if they'd all been paged.

"Fuck," Trace said into the phone. "This is all the department needs. Tell me the reporters don't already have it... Goddamnit... Yeah, he's sitting right here. Torres and Stern are, too... Fuck. Yeah, we're on it." He flipped his cell phone closed and scribbled an address on a napkin before saying, "Some fucking psychic got whacked. Reporters are already at the scene."

"Who's got the case?" Conner asked, beginning to stand.

"No determination yet. Dispatch patched me through to the Captain. He said since we're all together, we might as well go over and make it a dog and pony show for the press. Said he's got a bad feeling about this one."

"Are his feelings ever wrong?" Miguel asked.

Dylan shook his head. "When it comes to media nightmare, the Captain's got a nose that can smell the stink of one before anyone else can even see a cloud on the horizon."

"Shit," Miguel mumbled.

"Yeah, shit," Conner confirmed.

The scene was a circus. Reporters and television crews were camped near every black-and-white unit. A shout went up as soon as the detectives pulled in and within seconds their cars were mobbed.

"We heard there was a witness," a kid who looked like he was barely out of college yelled. "Has she been able to identify the killer?"

Another reporter, this one in need of deodorant, pressed a microphone into Trace's face, and said, "We heard that the department has a psychic on scene. Is this in response to the kidnapping case? Has the department decided to use them at murder scenes, too?"

Trace gritted his teeth and pushed the mike aside, just barely missing hitting the guy in the nose with it. A woman stepped forward but before she could get a question out, several uniformed officers moved in, ordering the reporters back and making a pathway for the homicide detectives.

A woman officer lifted the crime scene tape and they slipped under. One of the male cops followed them. When they were finally out of the reporters' sight, the uniformed cop said, "The Captain called ahead and said to be careful not to let the press get a hold of anything else. The coroner hasn't even hauled off the body and already there's a leak somewhere. Captain sounded like he was going to pop a blood vessel over this case."

"What gives? Is there a witness?" Miguel asked.

"Woman-friend of the victim. She probably got here just as the killer was finishing up. She's pretty shook up. Says she didn't see anything, but she thinks she heard a back door close. Neighbor's dog started barking about the same time, so it's likely the perp went out the back."

"Who's the vic?" Trace grunted as they stepped on the front porch.

"Guy by the name of Patrick Dean. Supposedly holds séances, among other things. Back door was unlocked, probably from the perp leaving. No sign of forced entry. Woman-friend said he was supposed to meet some important person tonight and asked her to be there, but she doesn't have any idea who he was meeting or what it was about. We've got her stashed in the kitchen. Captain wants us to find a way to keep her on ice. Cruiser went by her place. The media's already got it staked out. That's why the Captain's worried about a leak."

They got to the end of the hallway and halted at a blood-covered door. "Arterial spray," Trace said. "No sign of a struggle. Perp would have to be strong. Most likely a man. Doesn't feel like a woman's crime. Victim probably let his guest in, brought him down the hallway, but when they get to this point, the perp grabs the victim and slashes across his throat."

Conner grunted in response. Dylan and Miguel remained silent. The uniformed officer nodded, "Yeah, crime scene guys are inside. That was their read on it. Woman friend said the doorway to Dean's consultation room was partway open. She saw the blood and came in, but the vic was already dead."

Dylan frowned. "I wonder if the perp left the door open so he'd know if anyone came in, or whether the lady-friend just got lucky and he had enough time to escape without killing her."

The cop shrugged. "You guys need latex gloves?"

"Yeah," Dylan answered. The uniformed officer pulled a baggie containing gloves out of his pocket and passed them around.

As soon as the detectives were wearing the latex, the cop pushed open the door. "This is how we found him."

"Christ," Trace muttered.

The victim was lying on a cloth-covered table, his throat gaping from a single slashing wound, blood pooling and congealing on the dark red cloth beneath him. He was surrounded by white candles and positioned so that his arms folded and crossed on his chest. A sparkling crystal orb rested in the space between his hands.

"Fuck," Conner said, "I got a bad feeling about this."

They went over the scene, then every other room except the kitchen, but didn't find anything. "Damn," Miguel said. "Would have been nice if we could have wrapped this up by finding an appointment book telling us who he was meeting."

Conner grunted. "Maybe we can get something from the girlfriend."

They made the walk down to the kitchen and pushed in. Trace caught sight of Aislinn and felt like somebody'd just kicked him in the gut with steel-toed boots. Miguel muttered, "Shit," as all four detectives came to a halt just inside the doorway.

Aislinn's wide, deer-in-the-headlights look said she felt the same way at seeing them. Dylan said, "Maybe you'd better let us handle this, Trace."

Now that the shock had passed, a hot fury was washing through Trace. She'd left him to come see some other man? "Fuck, no," he growled and pushed forward, feeling a primitive satisfaction when she pressed back against her seat as he drew near. Yeah, she better be worried. She belonged to him.

The thought was like a blast of ice-cold water. What the fuck was wrong with him?

"What are you doing here?" Trace growled.

Aislinn's lips trembled. Her gaze swung to the other detectives and Trace wanted to grab her and make her face him.

Conner put a hand on Trace's arm and said, "Back off," and it was all he could do to keep from taking a swing at his friend. Christ, he felt like a rabid dog.

Out of the corner of his eye, Trace saw the uniformed cop who'd been babysitting shift away from the counter and take a step toward the kitchen table where Aislinn was.

Fuck, he needed to get himself under control. Trace pulled out a chair and sat down, crowding close enough to Aislinn that their knees almost touched. She moved away slightly, which had Trace stuffing his hands into his jacket pockets to keep from hauling her right up against him.

The other three detectives pulled out chairs but gave Aislinn some space. She shivered and said, "I already told the other officers everything I know."

Miguel leaned forward, puppy dog eyes offering comfort, and Trace gritted his teeth against the urge to push Miguel back. "We'll try and make this quick so we can get you out of here," Miguel said as he pulled a small notebook out of his pocket and put it down on the table.

Aislinn's eyes followed the notebook and stayed lowered. "How long have you known the victim?" Miguel asked.

"Patrick," she whispered. "His name is Patrick. I've known him for about seven months."

"He was your boyfriend?" Miguel asked and her eyes flew to his face, then to Trace's before shifting back to Miguel's.

"No. Just a friend."

"He advertised himself as a psychic?" Conner asked.

Aislinn gave a subdued nod.

Trace growled, "Where'd you meet him?"

"He came to the shop one day, to look at crystals."

Trace leaned forward, crowding further into Aislinn's space. Smelling some other man's cologne coming off her body, seeing her huddled in some other man's jacket, even if it probably belonged to one of the uniformed cops, wasn't helping to calm the fury that raged through his body at finding her here. "And you went out with him?"

"No. We were just friends."

Trace took his own jacket off, then without a word grabbed her arm and pulled the offending jacket off her and wrapped his own in its place. Dylan cleared his throat. Conner muttered "shit" under his breath. Miguel shook his head and tried to get back on track. "Do you have any idea who Dean was meeting tonight?"

"No. He told me that this meeting could open the world for him and asked me to be here, for moral support."

"What does 'open the world for him' mean?" Dylan asked.

"I don't know," Aislinn said.

Dylan persisted. "If you were to guess, what do you think Dean meant by it?"

Aislinn's brows drew together. "He might have meant that he was meeting an important client. Or he might have simply meant that a skilled teacher was considering taking him on as an apprentice."

Trace snorted but held his tongue. Conner sent him a look then asked, "What would Patrick normally do for a client?"

Aislinn's wary gaze swung to Trace, then Dylan, before she answered. "Sometimes he helped them find missing items. Or people. Sometimes remains if the people were dead."

Conner leaned forward. "Was that all he did?"

Aislinn gave a small negative shake of her head. "He held séances."

Trace started cursing under his breath. Aislinn tightened the jacket around herself, trying to keep from shaking. She needed to leave, to get away from the horror of finding Patrick murdered, to escape from Trace and the pain that seemed to splinter her heart in his presence.

"I'd like to go home now," she said.

Miguel folded his notebook and gave her a compassionate look. "The reporters have your place staked out. What about staying with one of your friends?"

"I can go to Sophie's."

"We'll give you an escort," Conner volunteered as the men stood.

Before Aislinn could say anything, Trace's steel grip wrapped around her upper arm, guiding her from her chair to stand next to him. "I'll take care of her."

Conner started to say something, but the expression on Trace's face stopped him. Dylan didn't have any qualms, though. "Fuck, Trace, the Captain's already tight-assed about this case. I'll make sure she gets to Sophie's house."

Trace didn't bother answering except to say, "I'll talk to you guys in the morning," as he guided Aislinn toward the kitchen door.

"Shit," Dylan muttered, moving forward. "We'll cover you."

They moved swiftly down the hallway, but stopped at the front door so that the four detectives could surround Aislinn. "Keep your head down," Trace said as he reached over and pulled his jacket up so that it covered her hair and shielded her face.

The walk down the driveway was done quickly. When Aislinn tried to stop at her car, Dylan said, "It'll have to stay here for now. We'll have it taken down to the station."

They cleared the shrub-shrouded driveway and reporters surged forward, flashbulbs firing in a steady stream. The uniformed officers held them back as the detectives got Aislinn to Trace's car. "Stay down," he ordered, pulling away from the curb and leaving the scene as fast as he could. She huddled for several blocks before some of the tension left Trace's body and he said, "It should be okay now."

Aislinn sat up and cast a quick glance at Trace. "If you have a cell phone, I'll call Sophie."

Trace clenched his teeth and tried to force some calm into his thoughts. Christ, how did she manage to make him feel so out of control? His cock was rock-hard and his brain just wanted to shut down for the night instead of trying to sort through a bunch of conflicting ideas. He should never have taken her back into the bar. He should have put her in his car after they'd fucked on the beach and taken her home right then and fucked her some more.

But now she was involved in this psychic mess, and skittish again, and he didn't want to fight with her. All he wanted to do was get her somewhere safe and… He took a deep breath and tried to stop the flood of fantasies that suddenly began washing through his brain. Shit, she was making him crazy.

Trace eased the car over to the curb and turned off the engine. Aislinn tensed but didn't grab for the door handle and try to bolt out of the car. He figured that had to be a good sign.

He slipped from behind the wheel and reached for her, trying to be slow and gentle, and reassuring. As his hands settled on her arms and pulled her toward him, he whispered, "I need to hold you, baby," and was shocked to realize that the words were true.

Aislinn felt the same beguilement spreading through her that she'd experienced at the bar. She wanted to resist his touch, but she couldn't. His body heat surrounded her, chasing away the terrible chill that had settled in her core. She let him pull her into his arms, cuddling closer as he slipped his hand underneath the jacket he'd wrapped her in and stroked along her spine.

Trace groaned against her hair as a multitude of unfamiliar sensations bombarded his system. He was rock-hard, but for once he was content just to hold a woman in his arms, rather than move directly into foreplay.

He moved so that he could press his lips against the soft skin of Aislinn's neck. She shivered and pressed closer to him. "I'm sorry you had to find your friend like that," Trace whispered.

"Do you think you'll find whoever killed Patrick?"

"I don't know. We'll do our best."

"Even if he was a psychic?"

Trace rubbed his chin against her silky hair as his arms tightened in reaction. "Let's not go there, baby."

Some of the warmth Aislinn had been experiencing seeped away. She tried to pull back but Trace wouldn't let her. "Patrick didn't have as much talent as he wanted, but he was able to help some people. He wasn't a con artist or a whacko."

Trace sighed and hugged Aislinn tighter. Christ, he didn't want to get into a fight about this with her. He wanted to take her home, put her in his bed, and fuck her until he fell asleep.

If the Captain's bad feeling about this case was right, then the shit was going to hit the fan tomorrow and keep hitting it. Trace figured he'd be lucky to get any time in the sack at all, for sleeping or fucking.

"It wouldn't matter if your friend was a crook, we'd still look for his killer." Trace let her loose but kept one arm around her shoulders, holding her next to him as he slid back behind the steering wheel.

Aislinn's heart thundered in her chest, at war with itself. It would be wiser, safer to go to Sophie's apartment. But each time she thought to save herself from pain, to open her mouth and demand that Trace take her there, a lonely ache ripped through her, stripping her defenses so that all she wanted was to spend the night wrapped in the warmth of Trace's arms.

Trace didn't look at the speedometer once, though he could tell by feel that he was well past the limit. All he could think about was getting Aislinn to his house before she got skittish again and demanded that he take her to Sophie's.

He'd been too long without and the sex on the beach had been incredible. That's the only reason he could come up with for his behavior, for this obsession with Aislinn. Christ, he was in for it. Even if the Captain didn't get wind of this, Dylan and the other guys in his department were going to give him a load of shit.

Trace hit the remote and watched with satisfaction as the garage door opened. Another second and he'd have Aislinn where he needed her.

Aislinn tensed as Trace drove into the garage and cut the motor. Doubt rushed in, threatening to overwhelm her. But Trace didn't allow her any escape. He simply pulled her along with him as he got out of the car and stepped into the house.

There was only a brief impression of pale blue walls and warm wooden floors before he pressed her back against the smooth stucco and leaned into her, biting and sucking at her mouth so that she would open for him.

His hand burned through her dress as he stroked across a nipple that had become stiff and painful. She whimpered and moved into Trace, unable to control or deny the need that made her want to open herself to him. His tongue slid inside her mouth, brushing and teasing against hers until they were both out of breath.

"I can't get enough of you," he whispered. "Right now it's all I can do to keep from taking you against the wall."

Aislinn's cunt throbbed at the heat of his words, at the fierce desire she saw in his face. "Take me that way," she whispered, and a thrill rushed up her spine as his face tightened and his eyes darkened.

Trace shuddered. He felt like an addict in need of a fix. He hadn't planned on dragging her into his house and jumping her right away. But now…now all he could think about was getting inside her tight wet sheath and making her whimper with pleasure.

Every sound he drew from her pulsed straight through him, swelling his dick and tightening his balls in a blend of pleasure and pain like nothing he'd ever experienced before. "Unzip me," he growled, his body tight with unbearable tension.

Trace's demand shot right to Aislinn's core. Her heartbeat skittered in an erratic beat. It unnerved her how much she liked his dominance. And yet his very desire for her made her feel safe.

"Unzip me," he growled again, this time accompanying the command with a small bite to her neck as he stripped her of her panties.

Aislinn slid her hands down his waist, marveling in the tight, firm feel of him, at the way he seemed to hold himself completely still, waiting for her to unzip his pants and touch him. Her fingers were unsteady as they trailed across his flat stomach and settled at the front of his jeans. Trace shuddered and pressed his thick, heavy, cloth-covered erection against her palm. She looked up at him and felt her heart open itself once again. She was already swollen and wet, so needy that she wanted to spread her legs and feel him inside her.

"Don't make me ask again," he said and she did as he commanded, opening the zipper and sliding his jockeys down so that she could wrap one hand around his engorged penis and cup the other under his testicles.

Trace groaned and bucked against her in response. A feminine thrill of power raced through Aislinn. "Guide me in," he said, his voice a rough growl as he easily lifted her so that her vagina was aligned with the cock she held captive.

Aislinn whimpered and watched as his face tightened. "Now," he said and she wrapped her legs around his waist, easing the tip of him into her wet, swollen sheath.

One of Trace's arms slid down to pull her more tightly against him as he plunged the rest of the way in. "Christ, you're so small. So tight." He pulled out, only to press forward again and again.

Aislinn arched against him each time he tried to pull out, tightening involuntarily, as though her body couldn't stand to be without his. His breathing was harsh. "You're killing me," he said and she shivered in response.

She needed him. All of him. Her mouth sought his and he answered her need, pressing wet, full lips against hers, stroking his tongue into her, dominating and yet providing a safe place for her. Aislinn responded by pressing more tightly against him so that each stroke sent a fiery pleasure through her.

His movements became fiercer, more possessive, as though he wouldn't accept anything less than her total surrender. Aislinn couldn't resist him, didn't want to. With a sob she gave herself up to him, taking his hot seed as an orgasm raged through her like an exploding star.

She was so weak that she didn't think she could stand, not that she had to. Trace's heart beat in a steady rhythm against her body as he carried her into the bedroom at the end of the hallway and gently laid her down on a bed before undressing her. She opened her eyes and was flooded by warmth at the tenderness and caring she saw on his face. Hope took hold of her, allowing the impossible dreams to once again take root in her heart.

The expression on her face should have terrified him. Instead, Trace alternated between wanting to hold Aislinn and wanting to go down on her, kissing every inch of her body until she was writhing underneath him and begging him to fuck her. Jesus. She was making him crazy.

He wanted to lock her in his house and never let her leave. And *that* scared the shit out of him.

"You okay?" he asked. He couldn't keep the masculine satisfaction out of his voice.

Warm heat flooded Aislinn's face along with pride. She'd pleased him, and that pleased her. "I'm fine."

He stripped off the rest of his clothes and joined her in bed, pulling her close before sliding the covers over them and turning off the light. Aislinn snuggled against him, soaking in his warmth. His hand stroked down her back, comforting her, coaxing her heart to throw away years of rejection and open to him. For the first time since her father had died and her secure world had been ripped apart, Aislinn felt like she belonged.

But then her mind wandered back to the events of the evening—to the bar, the beach, to Trace's reaction afterwards...to Patrick. Tears formed again and leaked down her cheeks. She focused her pain on Patrick. He hadn't deserved to die like that. Maybe if she'd just gotten there earlier... Her body shuddered.

Trace hugged her tighter. Christ, she was tearing him apart with her tears. His heart felt like somebody had a death grip on it. She seemed so fragile, so breakable. "Baby, please stop crying," he whispered against her hair. "You're going to make yourself sick if you don't get some sleep. Just let it go, Aislinn. We'll try and find out who murdered your friend."

The tears didn't stop immediately. And even when they did and her body relaxed into sleep, Trace continued to run his fingers through her silky hair and along the smooth skin of her back.

Fuck. He was in big trouble now.

* * * * *

Trace half expected the guys to razz him when he walked into the homicide section. The silence that greeted him instead was almost deafening.

Dylan was the first to look up. He shook his head and said, "Captain wants us in his office in ten minutes. The press has been crawling up his ass all morning. They got an anonymous tip that Patrick Dean was the psychic involved in the missing kid case."

"Fuck," Trace said. "Can this get any worse?"

A uniformed officer walked in. "Where's Aislinn?" she asked, practically scalding him with her frown.

It took him a minute to recognize Storm. "I left her at my place. Sleeping."

"You should have taken her to Sophie's. The last thing Aislinn needs right now is to be fucked and shown the door."

"That's between Aislinn and me."

"Yeah, well, I didn't mean for you to get involved with her. I thought she'd hit it off with Conner."

"Tough." Trace's gut clenched at the thought of Aislinn being anywhere else, with anyone else. He gritted his teeth. Last night he'd hardly been aware of Storm, and before that, he'd seen her around, enough to know that Miguel had it bad for her, but he didn't really know her very well. And right now he didn't think he wanted to. "Don't you have a beat to patrol?"

Conner choked on the coffee he was drinking. "Hey, let's go easy on each other. We've got plenty of other people wanting to rip into us."

Storm looked like she wanted to say something scathing. Instead she said, "Is she okay?"

Trace shifted uncomfortably, thinking about Aislinn crying herself to sleep. "She was sleeping. I didn't wake her up." He shot a look to Dylan.

Dylan stood up. "We got bigger problems right now. The press is still swarming on Inner Magick. Half of them think Aislinn's a witness. The rest of them think she's a psychic helping us. Now we've just got to pray no one comes up with a photo of her. The Captain would have our asses if the press finds out she was with us in the bar last night."

Miguel walked in, did a double take when he saw Storm, then grinned. "Couldn't stay away, huh?"

She wrinkled her nose. "Right."

Conner stood. "Time to go. You, too, Miguel, I'll fill you in on the way up to the Captain's office."

Miguel shot a quick look at Trace, before focusing on his partner. "Shit. About last night?"

"About the Dean case, yeah." Conner said. "The Captain doesn't know all of it. Yet. We'd better figure out what to tell him by the time we get to his office."

Chapter Three

☜

Aislinn shivered as she came awake, wanting the events of last night to be a wonderful dream followed by a terrible nightmare. But the fact that she was here, in Trace's home, in his bed, surrounded by echoes of his presence, told her that it had happened. All of it.

The silence and stillness let her know that Trace was gone. Though she knew he intended that she stay, she couldn't. She needed to think, to distance herself—to aid Patrick's spirit.

The phone on the table next to the bed offered a means of escape. She reached for it and called Sophie.

"Tell me where you are and I'll come get you!" Sophie said as soon as she heard Aislinn's voice.

"I'm at Trace's house."

"I know that, but so far no one has been willing to say exactly where that is! I've already called Storm three times trying to get the address. The last time I did she said she was getting ready to go into a meeting with the Captain and the rest of those macho Rambos."

Aislinn laughed softly. "I'm not even sure what part of the city I'm in. I'll go look for an address and call you back."

"Don't hang up! I've been up all night worried about you! It's been all over the news about Patrick." Sophie took a deep breath. "I'm sorry, Aislinn. I know he was your friend. Was it…terrible?"

Aislinn closed her eyes briefly. The picture of Patrick as the killer had laid him out was burned into her memory. "Yes," she whispered.

"Okay, I knew that. Get Trace's address and I'll be right over."

Aislinn's heart warmed at the demand in her friend's voice. Until Sophie had come into Moki's shop to look at crystals, Aislinn hadn't had a friend her own age — not since she was a small child, not since her mother had taken her to Elven-space.

"Okay, it may take a few minutes. I'm still in the bedroom."

Sophie gave a small laugh. "Stop. Don't go there. I want to hear all the details in person."

Aislinn smiled and put the phone down. There was no discarded mail in the bedroom so she moved into the hallway. The hardwood flooring and throw rugs were warm against her bare feet, the pale blue walls with pastel abstracts offered tranquility. Even in his absence, Trace's home was comforting, welcoming.

The homes of both her mother's father and her mother's Elf-lord heartmate had been the homes of royalty. So many of the rooms had been off-limits to a small mixed-blood child with no magic. "What happens if you break something? Can you repair it? Can you replace it with something of even greater value? It's best you not call attention to the magic you lack. Go now, don't let them find you in here. You'll only be punished," the lower-caste elves would say as they shooed her away.

Elf magic was the magic of beauty. Some could find precious gems and metals. Some could craft those gems and metals into jewelry and objects of great value. Some could create tapestries or art that shone more beautiful than the sun. Some could take spoken words or musical notes and combine them so the heart sang with joy.

She'd prayed for magic, hoped that it would come when she got older, and it had. But her magic was not a magic with value in Elven-space.

Aislinn ran a finger along the soft couch before sitting down on it to go through a stack of magazines on the coffee table. At the bottom of the pile she found an address adhered to a front cover and returned to the bedroom, reading it off to Sophie.

"I'm on my way," Sophie said.

Aislinn showered and got dressed, grimacing as she slipped on the dress she'd worn the previous evening. It would have to do until she got to Sophie's house. Thankfully she had some spare clothing there.

Her heart lurched when the doorbell rang. For a moment she regretted calling Sophie, regretted missing the chance to stay in Trace's home, to be here waiting for him when he returned. But it would be better, safer to her heart, to leave now, with a memory of his warmth and comfort held as a buffer against his earlier anger and rejection.

Now that some of the horror of discovering Patrick's murder had passed, now that the shock of having Trace come into her life had waned, she knew that she couldn't turn her back on her dead friend. She had skills, not valuable or useful in the eyes of her mother's people, but skills all the same that could help bring Patrick's killer to justice.

She made her way to the door and found Trace's note. *Stay inside. The security alarm is on and will go off if any of the doors or windows are opened. Help yourself to anything in the refrigerator. Trace.*

The doorbell sounded again, immediately followed by pounding and Sophie's yell. Aislinn smiled before calling out, "I'm right here, Sophie. He's got the alarm set. It'll take me a minute to disarm it."

From the other side of the door, Sophie laughed. "*That's* going to go over well."

Aislinn lightly ran her fingers over the alarm keypad. It was easy for her to read which numbers were touched regularly. The faint psychic particles left behind by Trace marked them, and with a little concentration she was able to differentiate the first and last numbers in the sequence. It took several tries to unlock the remaining code order and deactivate the alarm.

Sophie hurtled into the house and enveloped Aislinn in a tight hug as soon as the front door opened. "I've been so worried about you!"

Aislinn returned the hug just as fiercely. "I'm glad you're here."

Sophie hugged Aislinn once more for good measure. "Storm called as soon as she heard last night. She even went to Miguel's house and tried to get Trace's address from him. Not a chance, and you know how persuasive she can be. It's like those guys took an oath of silence and brotherhood or something! Let's get out of here before one of them does a drive-by to make sure you're still here."

Aislinn's chest tightened as she pulled away from Sophie. She'd only been in Trace's home a short while and yet it felt right, a safe and warm haven that welcomed her.

As if Sophie sensed the direction of her thoughts, she said, "Do *not* tell me you're thinking of staying here. Trust me on this, get some breathing room before you get in over your head with him."

Aislinn suspected it was already too late for that, but the part of her that tried to guard her heart from rejection and pain silently echoed Sophie's words. She nodded. "I've got to reset his alarm."

* * * * *

"I can tell by the looks on your faces that I'm not going to like what I hear," Captain Ellis said as the men and Storm filed into his office and took their seats. "Go ahead and spit it out."

Conner and Miguel shifted uncomfortably. Dylan looked to Trace, then answered the Captain. "The five of us were out for drinks at a place called Lily's last night. The woman who discovered Dean's body was with us."

The Captain's lips tightened. "Tell me the rest of it."

When none of the men volunteered, Storm said, "My cousin wanted me to set her and two of her friends up. I was thinking about hooking up with some guys from the gym I go to, but then Dylan said that Trace needed to get out of a rut and I thought, what could it hurt? Trace would probably hit it off with Sophie's friend, Tiffany." She frowned at Trace. "Only he went right for Aislinn instead. They danced. They went out on the beach for a while. They came back in."

The Captain closed his eyes briefly, then stared at Trace. "Tell me you kept it in your pants." He splayed his hands out in front of him. "Tell me that the sick feeling in my gut is from my wife's cooking and not from what I'm going to be reading in the newspaper. I'm seeing the story now. *Conspiracy uncovered. Cops murder psychic who showed the department up."*

Trace gritted his teeth. "Aislinn was just in the wrong place at the wrong time. I've got her on ice. The reporters aren't going to get to her. There's nothing to worry about, Captain."

"You've got her on ice?" Captain Ellis said through clenched teeth. "Where?"

"My place." Trace managed to keep his voice neutral despite the fierce wave of possessiveness that whipped through his body and right to his cock at the image of going home and finding Aislinn waiting for him—preferably in his bed.

"And you don't see a problem with that?" the Captain barked.

Dylan spoke up. "Captain, if we've got a leak in the department, having her on ice at Trace's place isn't a bad idea. Right now the only people who know where she is are in this room."

Storm said, "And my cousin. But Sophie won't talk."

Conner added, "It might work to our advantage since Aislinn works at Inner Magick. We could play it a couple of ways—she's a psychic helping us or a psychic in danger. Either way, we're serious about solving Dean's murder and keeping the city safe."

The Captain looked around at the men and woman in front of him. He was proud that they presented a united front, he'd been in tense situations like this before and had team members ripping into each other, but the feeling in his gut from last night was back full force. This was going to be a media nightmare. "Let's leave it for now," he said. "I guess you've heard that Patrick Dean was the psychic who supposedly helped find the Morrison kid? Well, you heard right. I talked to Bruner over in Missing Persons. The Morrisons screamed in his ear as soon as they heard that Dean had been killed."

Storm frowned and raised her hand. Captain Ellis nodded, giving the go-ahead to ask the obvious question. "How'd the media get the jump on that? Did Bruner know the name of the psychic who supposedly located the child?"

Captain Ellis' smile was grim. "Good question. Bruner says that he didn't know squat. Parents wouldn't tell him for fear of 'retribution' against the psychic. And the media—same old bullshit. Protected sources, yadda yadda yadda. You see where I'm going with this nightmare? Read the headlines—*Parents of kidnapped child feared police revenge when psychic was able to locate their son.* As of right now, this is case number one and you're all on it. Officer O'Malley is on loan. Use her for legwork. She's got an in with this psychic crowd. Use it. Use her to pull some information out of them. I have a feeling the rest of you are going to meet a wall of silence." His attention focused on Trace and some actual humor came to his eyes. "Strike that. Trace has an inside run on this, too. Maybe he'll be able to put his persuasive…uh…tool to good use. My gut tells me Aislinn Windbourne knows more than she's saying. See what you can get out of her. According to the first officer on the scene's report, they do it all at the place she's employed. Tarot cards, crystals, fortune-telling. The works."

Trace had managed to forget Aislinn's mention of meeting Dean over crystals, he'd managed to talk himself into the idea that Aislinn was just trying to be a good friend to Dean and support him morally, like she'd said the victim needed. The thought of Aislinn being involved in that psycho-psychic shit, of actually believing in it and peddling it, was enough to shrivel Trace's dick and kill a good hard-on. Or so he thought until anger flooded into him. Son of a bitch, he'd cure her of it even if he had to handcuff her to the bed and keep her there.

Those images poured blood right back into his cock. Christ, he should have known. She was so soft, so sensitive. She probably got into the stuff when she was in college or something, as a way to fit in. She needed somebody like him around to...

Fuck. What was he thinking? And why wasn't he in a panic?

His partner's snickering brought Trace back to the present. Conner and Miguel wore smirks. Even the Captain seemed ready to crack a smile. Only Storm surveyed him with an expression that was less than amused.

Captain Ellis said, "I'm going to leave it to you guys to make a plan and divide up the workload. Just keep me informed. The mayor's already called a press conference, Conner, why don't you be part of the dog and pony show? Let's break for now. Trace, stand by for a minute."

Trace stood, figuring if he was going to get his ass burned, he'd just as soon do it standing. The Captain steepled his fingers in front of him. As soon as the others were gone, he asked, "Is having you on this case going to be a problem for you, Trace?"

"No. It's not any different than having your wife come on a crime scene." Trace shoved his hands in his pockets. Fuck. Where did that come from?

The Captain raised his eyebrows. "Interesting that you're drawing a parallel with my wife. I'll leave you on the case...for now, only because my gut tells me it's the right thing to do. But if the shit starts hitting and it looks like the department—or you—are going to get covered in it, then I'll pull you. Understood?"

Trace nodded.

"Okay. Make sure you guys keep me up-to-date. And keep whatever you find close to you."

"You think there's a leak?"

The Captain shrugged. "Hell, I don't know and we don't have time to go looking. So we won't take any unnecessary chances. This thing stinks and we're only getting the first whiff of it."

* * * * *

"I drove by Inner Magick," Sophie said as they pulled away from Trace's house. "I wanted to get you some extra clothes and maybe a protection crystal. But there was a camera crew parked out front and a couple of cars out back that looked like they might have reporters in them." She cut a worried glance over at Aislinn. "It makes me nervous that they found out about you so quickly. Storm was upset about it, too. Everyone assumes that you scared the killer off. But Storm asked if maybe whoever killed Patrick knew that you were going to be there and wanted you to find the...Patrick."

Aislinn ran shaky fingers through her hair. "I don't know. I...what happened with Trace... I was...I wasn't...aware, the way I usually am. And then afterward I didn't touch anything." She gave Sophie a tentative smile. "Between the stories that Storm tells you and the

CSI that you always insist we watch, I knew better than to do anything that might destroy evidence." Aislinn took a deep breath and added, "But I want to go back to Patrick's house. I need to go back. Maybe there's something there that will help the police."

Sophie's fingers tightened on the steering wheel momentarily. "I'll go with you."

"You don't have to."

"I know." Sophie looked over at Aislinn. "I didn't like Patrick, but he didn't deserve this. I'll call Storm when we get to my place. She's probably the only cop on the force who has an open enough mind. When I talked to her this morning she was going in to see her captain. She was going to ask him to let her assist whoever got assigned the case — probably Trace and the rest of them."

Aislinn rubbed her hand against the fabric of her dress. Even after her shower, she could still smell Trace. "Tell her that it's better to go as soon as possible."

"The newspapers are claiming that Patrick was the psychic who helped find that kidnapped boy yesterday," Sophie said.

There was the hint of a question in Sophie's statement. Aislinn looked out of the window and tried to ignore it. Sophie had disliked Patrick from their first meeting, seeing him as someone who wanted to use Aislinn. It didn't help that Patrick had reciprocated the feeling, claiming that Sophie just wanted to hoard Aislinn's time and talent.

A loud sigh came from Sophie's direction. "Not that Trace's attitude wouldn't be enough to kill even the best after-sex buzz, but it was more than that last night at the bar, wasn't it? When you were so upset, I thought it was because Trace opened his mouth and was so rabidly negative about psychics. But it was more than that. You helped Patrick locate the Morrison boy, didn't you?"

"Yes," Aislinn admitted in a whisper.

"Do the parents know it was you and not Patrick?"

"I don't think they know. Patrick had a baseball mitt that belonged to the boy, Thad. He told the parents that he needed some time to meditate before he could consult with them."

"You mean he needed time to bring the glove to you. Where did you meet him?"

"At the shop. We did a session in the back room, then he called the parents and left to meet them. They called the police, then went to where their son was being kept."

Sophie groaned. "And the man who had taken the boy just happened to escape, but no one can identify him. Doesn't that seem…convenient?" She sighed in frustration. "Do you think maybe it was faked, possibly so that Patrick would have more credibility? Doesn't it seem odd to you that right after Thad Morrison is rescued, Patrick suddenly has an important meeting, but he needs you for moral support? Maybe he was afraid that whoever he was meeting with was going to ask him to prove himself by finding someone else who was missing."

"Sophie," Aislinn chided quietly, "the boy's kidnapping wasn't a hoax. I could follow the trail of his fear and pain. I could sense his parent's anguish on the glove."

"Okay," Sophie conceded, "but you need to tell Storm that you were the one who really located Thad Morrison, just in case Patrick's death has something to do with that case."

Aislinn shivered as Trace's image flashed through her mind. A fist squeezed around her heart as she remembered his fury. *Christ, I hate that psychic bullshit. I'd like to lock every single one of them up. They're all either con artists or whackos.*

* * * * *

Trace joined the rest of the guys, and Storm, in the bullpen. He wasn't thrilled by her presence but he could tell he was in the minority. Miguel was smiling like a kid at Christmas time, focusing on the uniformed cop like a puppy in front of its food dish. Conner and Dylan were leaning forward, expressions serious, concentrating on whatever she was saying.

"You still on the case?" Dylan asked.

"Yeah. I miss anything here?" Trace pulled up a chair and joined them at Conner's desk.

Miguel said, "Storm wants to escort Aislinn back to the scene."

Trace tensed. "No."

Conner cleared his throat. "Might not be a bad idea, Trace. Right now we don't know jack shit about this stuff. We can't tell if anything's missing or different. Aislinn might be able to."

Trace clenched his teeth. "I don't want Aislinn involved in this any more than she has to be. You have questions, fine. I'll bring her in or you can come by my place and talk to her. But she stays on ice."

Conner cut a look over to Dylan for support. Trace's partner said, "Look, Trace, she was friends with the guy. End of story. You don't have to get your dick in a twist about it. But unless we can find someone else who's familiar with Dean's séance room, then Aislinn might be the only one who can help us."

Rage boiled through Trace. God, he hated this stuff. But if he wasn't careful, he was going to get himself kicked right off the case. One way or another this murder threatened to bust his balls. "Fine. One visit. I'll escort her. Then I want her kept as far away from this crazy psychic shit as she can get."

Dylan threw his hands up. "Fine. Fine. But maybe someone else ought to take her in. You're not exactly…"

Trace cut him off. "My way. I'm not letting her walk in there without me."

Conner and Dylan exchanged glances. Conner finally shrugged. "Okay, Trace." He looked down at his watch. "I've got to head back to the Captain's office to get ready for this dog and pony show. How do you want to tackle this?"

Storm stared at Trace. "I'm going to Patrick's house with Aislinn and the caveman here."

There were snickers from the other guys and a glare from Trace. "I'll go with Trace and Storm," Miguel said, "then hook up with Conner afterward."

Dylan shot a look at Trace before saying, "I'll canvas Dean's neighbors then I can tackle the Morrisons. It still stinks like a publicity stunt, but Dean turning up dead doesn't feel like a coincidence. I'll try and shake it out of them how the reporters found out that Dean was connected to them."

"Just go easy," Trace said. "The Captain has never been wrong. He thinks we're just getting the first whiff of stink. The last thing we need is to have the news screaming about us harassing parents who had a missing kid."

Dylan grunted. "Yeah, tell me about it. God I hate this psychic bullshit. Just give me a straight up murder any day. Jealous spouse. Greedy partner. Mob hit. Anything's better than this."

The detectives laughed and started to push their chairs away from the desk. Storm held a hand up to halt them. "Look, maybe we'd better get this on the table right now. If I'd known you guys were so rabid about anything you can't put in an evidence bag, I'd never have introduced you to Sophie and Aislinn last night. Not that I understand the hocus-pocus stuff, or believe in all of it, but there *are* things that can't be explained, like cop hunches and the Captain's gut feeling for public relations nightmares. Whether you guys want to believe it or not, some psychics aren't fakes." She frowned at Trace. "And whether The Caveman accepts it or not, Aislinn is involved in this. She not only knows a lot about this stuff, but she's got…talents that can't be explained away."

Storm paused, wishing she had a crowbar so she could pry some closed minds open, but figuring she was doing what she could. Damn! She wished like anything that she'd gone to the gym and hooked up with some of the guys there rather than agreeing to try and set Trace up. It had never crossed her mind that he'd get a hard-on for Aislinn. She'd have bet money that the chemistry would have meshed between him and Tiffany, if it meshed with anyone.

"Aislinn can help us. But she's…cautious and sensitive." Storm looked at each of the homicide detectives before settling on Trace again. "If you guys keep up with the attitude, then you're going to shut her down. Then it'll be ten times harder solving this case. Besides that, she's like a sister to Sophie. I don't want to see Aislinn hurt or abused. That's all. I just wanted to get it out on the table. If you don't want to have to deal with the 'psychic bullshit', then let me be the liaison with Aislinn. I'll give her a fair deal."

Miguel spoke up, shooting Storm a grin. "Bring it on. I can handle it."

Conner grunted and looked at Trace. "There's plenty of work for everyone. I'm fine with leaving Aislinn to Storm."

Dylan shrugged. "Fine by me."

Trace gritted his teeth as all eyes turned to him. He knew they all wanted him to back off. He couldn't. His cock was rock-hard. His skin felt like it was about to peel off his body. He needed to get back to his place and fuck Aislinn. He needed to hear her whimpers as he took her. He needed to feel her body writhe under him as he pounded into her hot little cunt. "You want to be the one who talks to Aislinn about this shit, fine, but I'm going to be with you." He stood and stalked out, needing a few minutes to pull it together before they went to get Aislinn. Christ, he'd never felt so out of control.

He left the building, heading for the Starbucks out of habit. Dylan caught up with him halfway down the block. "Trace…"

"Fuck, just leave it alone."

"Look…"

Trace stopped and turned toward Dylan, ready to…shit, he didn't know what he was going to do, but the look on his partner's face shut some of what he was feeling down. "I'm dealing with it, okay."

Dylan held his hands up in surrender. "Sure. Sure. Anything you say. You going for coffee?"

"Yeah." It came out sounding harsh.

Dylan tried to lighten the mood. "You want me to walk ten paces behind you?"

Trace exhaled loudly. "No."

They continued down the street in silence until they got to Starbucks and Dylan said, "Hey, I thought Commander Joe was settled in at the homeless shelter."

Trace followed Dylan's gaze and saw a familiar figure pushing a shopping cart full of clothing, blankets, and dumpster treasure. "Fuck."

Dylan shook his head. "You want the usual?"

"Yeah," Trace said, already moving toward the homeless man.

Commander Joe stopped pushing the cart as Trace drew closer. There was a momentary look of confusion and suspicion before the man's face cleared. "Oh, it's you. I've got some pretty things to show you. Picked them up this morning."

"What are you doing here, Joe? You're supposed to be at Sunlight House."

The man's smile faltered and his hand reached for the small American flag that was pinned to the lapel of his tattered jacket. "This is my route. Someone else will get it if I'm away too long. I already lost my place under the bridge." He started digging around in one of the garbage bags and pulling out old pieces of jewelry. He lined them up on top of a blanket. "These would make a nice gift."

Trace closed his eyes briefly, already knowing that it was futile. Hell, he'd gotten Joe into three shelters in the last six months, but he never stayed. "Sunlight House is a lot safer. There's been some violence against people living on the streets. I can call for a patrol car to give you a lift back to the shelter."

"No. No. I can't hear myself think there. Walls keep closing in on me. Guy in the bed next to me was having flashbacks. It's better out here."

Dylan appeared with three cups of coffee and a bag. He handed one to Trace and offered a second to Commander Joe, along with the bag. "Got a bear claw, if you're interested."

The homeless man took the coffee and the bag. He waved his hand over the assortment of jewelry. "Take one."

Dylan shook his head. "Don't have a girlfriend to give it to." But when Commander Joe tried to give the coffee and pastry back to him, Dylan relented and picked up a ring with a clear green stone in its center. "You waiting on a ride back to the shelter?"

The homeless man's face tightened into stubborn lines. "No. I'm not going back there. Nobody can make me go back there." He carefully placed the coffee and the bag with the pastry into his shopping basket, before gripping the handle so tightly that his knuckles showed white against the faded and cracked red plastic. "I've got to finish my route now," he said and moved away from Trace and Dylan.

Dylan pocketed the ring and looked at Trace, glad to see that his partner seemed to be back in control of himself, glad to see that Trace was handling the fact that Commander Joe was back on the street again.

Dylan shook his head against the hopelessness of it all. Commander Joe never stayed in a shelter for very long. Hell, none of the Vietnam vets that ended up on the streets did, but Trace kept trying anyway. Maybe it was just habit, something Trace had grown up being involved in, or maybe some part of Trace hoped that if one of them could be turned around, then his uncle could be, too—but there was no way Dylan was going to touch that one. "You ready to head back?"

Trace turned away from the sight of the homeless man pushing his basket full of possessions down the sidewalk. His thoughts shifted to Aislinn and his cock responded instantly. "Yeah, let's go."

* * * * *

"They're still here," Sophie said as she drove past the front entrance of Inner Magick and then around the building to the back stairs leading up to Aislinn's apartment. "I didn't really think they'd give up, but I was hoping."

Aislinn shivered at the sight of the reporters. She'd known they were here, but actually seeing them sent her heart racing with fear. She had few Elven privileges, yet most of their laws applied to her. If her mother's people thought that their existence might be discovered, then they could order Aislinn to leave, to never again have contact with Sophie, or Moki…or Trace.

A sharp pain shimmered through her at the prospect of losing those she loved. Even before the testing and the banishment, she'd been alone. She couldn't bear the thought of once again having no one who cared for her.

"They'll go away once the murderer is found," Aislinn said, knowing that no matter how difficult it would be to return to Patrick's house, to touch his belongings, she would do it.

* * * * *

Trace couldn't believe it. She was gone.

He'd walked through the house twice before stopping at the alarm console for a third time. Fuck. How the hell had she gotten out of his house? Dylan and Conner were the only two people who knew the code besides him. Neither of them would have revealed it.

The system was armed when Trace walked in. He'd had to disarm it. His gut told him that she hadn't slipped out while he was looking for her. The note he'd left warning her not to leave was still attached to the back of the front door.

Trace punched in his code and reactivated the alarm before walking the perimeter of the house to check for signs that she'd gone out a window while he was looking for her. Nothing. He was never going to live this down.

Storm and Miguel had gotten out of the car and were leaning against the doors. Trace gritted his teeth and asked, "Did Aislinn come out?"

Miguel frowned. "No, was she supposed to?"

Storm's barely suppressed smile made Trace's jaw clench even tighter. He wasn't going to give her the satisfaction of asking if she knew how Aislinn could have gotten out of an alarmed building. "Let's head to Sophie's," he said, angling for the driver's seat just as Storm's cell phone rang. He heard her say, "I'm with Trace and Miguel. We're on our way there now. How's she holding up?... Do you think she can do it?... See you in a few."

* * * * *

Sophie put down the phone. "They're on the way. Are you sure you're up to this?"

Aislinn ran her fingers along the smooth edge of a dark, smoky crystal, wishing that she could pull its timeless tranquility into herself. "Yes. I've got to. Who's with Storm?"

Sophie sat down next to Aislinn. "Trace and Miguel."

Aislinn looked away. Dread and anticipation swirled in equal measure inside her chest. The things in herself that she valued the most, Trace would never believe existed. He despised anyone who claimed to be psychic. And yet when he was near, she craved his touch. He beguiled her. Against a background of loneliness and pain, she wanted to believe that he was the one she was destined to form a heartbond with. But how could she be sure that it wasn't just human lust and not the compelling need that the Elven had to touch their mates?

Sophie picked up a flat green crystal from the collection on her coffee table and said, "Are you okay with seeing Trace so soon?"

"I'll have to be. I need to do this for Patrick."

But it didn't stop Aislinn's heart from tightening when there was a perfunctory knock at Sophie's door before Storm pushed in, followed by the two homicide detectives.

Storm rushed over and pulled Aislinn to her feet, hugging her tightly. "I wish I'd been there last night when the call came in!"

Aislinn returned the hug, feeling the anger radiating off Trace's body as he stopped next to her. As soon as Storm let go, Trace grabbed Aislinn's arms and pulled her around to face him. "You were supposed to stay at my house."

She stiffened against his restraint, against the need that built whenever he touched her. "I didn't know when you'd be back. There are things I have to do. For Patrick."

Trace gritted his teeth. "You're not going to Dean's house without me. And you're not staying here. As soon as we're done, you're going back to my place." He pulled her close enough that their bodies touched.

Aislinn shivered in response to the naked desire burning in his eyes, to the hard cock that burned through cloth and imprinted itself on her abdomen, at the raw possessiveness in his tone. When he moved closer and covered her lips with his, she was lost. There was no thought to resist the demand of his tongue as it thrust into her mouth and stroked over hers. She melted against him, wanting nothing more than to let him take control.

Fire raced through Trace's dick as Aislinn's soft body molded itself to his. Fuck. Her submissiveness was an aphrodisiac that shot his control to hell. He should never have started this. But now that he had, he couldn't stop thrusting his tongue in and out of her mouth. Christ, he wanted to do the same thing with his cock. When he got her home... Trace groaned as erotic images of Aislinn sucking him deep into her mouth made his balls pull up tight against his body. When she whimpered it took everything he had to keep from pushing her down to her knees so that she could give him relief.

Miguel's voice pushed through the haze of lust in Trace's mind. "Maybe we should leave them alone for a few minutes, let them get it out of their systems before we head out to Dean's place."

Aislinn stiffened and pulled back from the kiss. Satisfaction surged through Trace at the sight of her flushed face and swollen lips, at her dazed expression. "Let's get this over with," he growled.

* * * * *

Miguel and Trace both cursed as they neared Patrick's house. The reporters hadn't given up their vigil.

"Stay out of sight," Trace told Aislinn. "You, too, Sophie, unless you want to be part of this media circus."

A uniformed officer got out of a nearby patrol car and walked over to where the crime scene tape was stretched across the driveway entrance. Trace slowed to a stop and rolled down his window. The cop nodded in acknowledgement, then did a double-take. "They move you to homicide, Storm?"

"Just on this one. Everything pretty quiet here?"

The cop snorted. "I wish. It's like watching a pack of hyenas. Anything moves and they're on it." He pointed down the street to where an unmarked police car was parked along the curb. "A couple of reporters from *The Daily* are tailing Trace's partner, probably trying to figure out which neighbors to hound for more hype. You want my opinion, we oughtta pull them in for obstructing justice."

Trace grunted. "Yeah, only problem is that it'd just add to their storylines. They'd love that. Either way, we're fucked."

The cop shook his head. "Yeah, we're fucked." He put his hand on the crime scene tape. "You going in?"

"Yeah," Trace said. "We've got a couple of civilians with us. Make sure the cameras stay back."

"No problem."

The cop pulled the tape away and Trace shot down the driveway, angling for a position that offered the most protection. His guts were churning, something that hadn't happened to him since he was a rookie. The lack of control pissed him off.

Storm turned to Aislinn. "Did you park in the driveway last night?"

Aislinn nodded.

Storm asked, "Can you take it from here? Tell us what you were sensing?"

"Christ!" Trace flung his door open and got out, leaving the disbelieving epithet hanging in the air behind him.

Aislinn's eyes watered, but she steeled herself against his rejection. She had survived worse. She had survived years of being an outcast among her mother's people.

Miguel muttered "shit" and cast a quick look toward Storm before following Trace out of the car. Storm shook her head. "Are you going to be able to do this with Trace here?"

Aislinn took a deep breath. "I have to."

Sophie gave her a hug. Storm squeezed Aislinn's hand. "Okay. Did you sense anything?"

Aislinn closed her eyes and forced herself to relive those moments outside of Patrick's house. Without conscious thought, her hand lifted and she ran a finger along the delicate wings on one of the butterfly earrings. She shuddered as the feelings of foreboding washed over her again. "I felt uneasy. Like I wanted to turn around and leave. I was afraid that Patrick was going to hold a séance."

"I thought he didn't do that when you were around!" Sophie interrupted, her voice angry.

"Sophie," Storm warned, motioning her cousin to stay quiet.

"He doesn't." Aislinn took a steadying breath and corrected herself. "He didn't. He knew that I wouldn't participate in trying to call spirits back from the dead."

"But you were worried that he was going to do it last night?" Storm asked softly.

Aislinn took a minute before answering. "No. I don't know why the thought came to me. Maybe he was already dead by then. Maybe that's why I felt so uneasy."

Storm nodded. "Anything else?"

"No."

"Okay, so you got out of the car and went to the front door. Anything there?"

"Just the same. Uneasiness."

"Are you sure you're up to doing it all over again?" Storm asked.

Aislinn opened her eyes and nodded before slipping out of the car. Her gaze flew to Trace. His face was rigid, his lips set in a tight line. When he made no move to touch her, Aislinn's heart lurched in her chest. She took a deep breath, turning away from him and walking the short distance to Patrick's front door. "The door was open, just a little bit," she said. "I pushed it wider but the hallway was dark."

Miguel spoke up for the first time. "Was the porch light on when you got here?"

"No. There were no lights on in the house."

"Son of a bitch," Trace muttered. "You went in anyway."

Two pairs of cop eyes glared at him to shut up. Aislinn whispered, "I gave my word that I'd be here."

"So you pushed the door open?" Storm asked.

Aislinn nodded and reached down to touch the doorknob. There was a residue of anticipation coating the smooth crystal, but she'd expected that. The crystal knob was one she'd selected for Patrick. She turned the knob and pushed the door open, bracing herself against the sight of the bloodstains on the wall. Next to her Sophie let out a small gasp before turning away.

Miguel said, "Maybe you'd better wait in the car."

"You don't have to come in, Sophie. I'll be okay," Aislinn said.

Sophie nodded and moved so that she didn't have to look at the spot where Patrick had probably been murdered. "Are you going to be okay?" Miguel asked Sophie. She waved him away, then bent over the railing and lost her breakfast. He hesitated before following the others inside.

Aislinn came to a halt at the doorway leading to Patrick's magic room. She could feel the force of Trace's disapproval pressing against her, seeming to demand that she not enter the room in front of her.

Among her mother's people, heartmates were two halves of a whole, a blend of opposites whose differences enhanced the whole, making the two more than they'd be as individuals.

Aislinn fought the urge to yield to Trace's silent demand, to his acknowledged dominance. "Just Storm," she whispered. "I only want Storm to go in with me."

"That's fine," Miguel said, shifting so that he stood behind Aislinn and blocked Trace from getting to the door.

There was a long tense moment of silence. A silent battle of wills between the three cops. Finally Storm said, "Go ahead when you're ready, Aislinn."

Aislinn pushed into Patrick's magic room and felt the breath seize in her chest as Patrick's presence surrounded her, overwhelmed her. When she would have stumbled forward, Storm caught her by the arm, steadying her.

"Take as much time as you need," Storm said. "You're cleared to touch anything you need to touch. And if something's missing, let me know, regardless of how small it is."

The pressure in Aislinn's chest eased slightly, as though Patrick's spirit recognized that it couldn't communicate with her directly, but she was still aware of its presence. She shivered and moved deeper into the room, glancing only briefly at the table where Patrick's corpse had been positioned, posed by whoever killed him. "He was holding the crystal he uses to scry with. Did they take it to the police station?"

Storm shrugged. "Probably."

Patrick's magic room also served as his den. Polished wooden shelves loaded with books on various occult disciplines lined one wall. A matching desk was discretely placed in a corner, its surface bare except for a small collection of strategically placed crystals. Patrick's spirit was an invisible force pushing Aislinn toward the desk. As soon as she stood next to it she knew that an arrangement of crystals set in a dragon-shaped silver holder was missing. It had been her gift to Patrick, to help him make the most of his psychic gifts.

"One of them is missing," Aislinn said. "Five crystals set in a holder shaped like a dragon."

Storm came over to stand next to Aislinn. "You're sure?"

"Yes."

"Any chance that Patrick broke it or loaned it out or put it somewhere else?"

Aislinn shook her head. "I don't think so."

"Where was it?"

Aislinn pointed to where the arrangement had been.

"Anything significant about it? Was it valuable?"

"Only to Patrick."

Storm nodded. "It's not uncommon for perps to take souvenirs from their victims. This might be important if we come up with a suspect. Do you think you could describe it in enough detail that an artist could draw it?"

"I've got drawings of it at the shop." She paused. "I made it for Patrick."

Storm's eyebrows rose. "You?"

"Yes."

"Do you make a lot of them?"

"No."

"Would the killer have known where the crystal came from? That it meant something special to Patrick?"

Aislinn moved her hand over the desk, at the seemingly random placement of the remaining crystals. "If the killer recognized that this is a mystical pattern, then he would know that the missing piece was the most important one."

Storm smiled with fierce satisfaction. Her cop instincts told her that the perp taking this particular souvenir was important. That meant he knew a hell of a lot about this stuff.

This was why she'd gone to the Captain and asked if she could help on the case. Some other cop, especially one who was rabidly anti-psychic, might not have gotten this out of Aislinn.

Aislinn took a steadying breath and dropped her hand to the surface of Patrick's desk. The energy from the remaining crystals hummed through her palm in an incomplete rhythm, but otherwise there was no malevolent force, no dark emotions left seething, even in the spot where the missing crystal had rested. With great care Aislinn went through Patrick's desk. Nothing resonated with any emotion until her hand brushed against a book and a foreign excitement—Patrick's excitement—raced through her, the force of it giving testament to the fact that he'd been handling the book recently. As soon as Aislinn passed the book to Storm, the force of Patrick's spirit stopped pressing down on her, becoming only a vague, fluttering presence.

"*Tales of a Psychic Investigator* by D. L. Lucca," Storm snorted. "Sounds like something from a tabloid publisher."

"This was important to Patrick. He was handling this before he died. He was excited." Storm gave her a questioning look, but there was nothing Aislinn could add. Feeling drained, she said, "I'm ready to leave now."

Storm's eyebrows came together. "You're sure? It may be tough to get back in here again."

Aislinn closed her eyes briefly. The weight of Patrick's spirit had lifted. "I'm sure."

* * * * *

Trace wanted to knock Miguel away from the door and follow Aislinn inside. Christ, he hated this. Hated that she was here now. Hated that she'd ever been here. Hated the fact that she was involved in the psychic mumbo jumbo. Hated the fact that despite all of it, he still wanted her.

Just being near Aislinn made him rock-hard—and more. As much as he'd like to tell himself that it was just lust, Trace was honest enough to admit that it wasn't just about fucking her. He felt possessive, primitive when he was around her, like it was a matter of life and death to get her back to his house.

He flicked a glance at his watch. She'd only been away from him for a few minutes but he felt like he could barely stand the separation much longer—not with her so close.

"Move," he told Miguel.

Miguel had the nerve to grin. "Man, you've got it bad."

Trace gritted his teeth. "This is bullshit. Get out of my way."

Miguel's eyes went serious. "Give it a few minutes, okay? What's it going to hurt?"

Trace moved a few steps closer, but before he reached Miguel the door to the séance room opened and Aislinn stepped out, followed by Storm. "Let's go," he said, taking Aislinn by the arm and pulling her up against his body.

Just the feel of her against his side brought some relief. She shivered and turned so that her face was pressed into his chest. Trace had to stifle a groan as she cuddled his cock against her belly. He couldn't keep from bending close, so that his face was next to hers. "I'll take you back to my house," he said as he placed a gentle kiss below her ear.

Aislinn denied the need to submit. How could he be her true heartmate when he rejected her ability? "I can stay at Sophie's apartment. There are things I need to do."

Trace's grip tightened on her. "Whatever you need to do, you can do it at my place."

Aislinn pulled away so that she could look at him. His heart tightened at the sadness he read in her eyes. She shook her head slightly. "I can't."

"You can. You will."

Aislinn steeled herself against his reaction, his rejection, but it was better to face it now and get it over with. "There are some crystals I'm working with, for clients."

Trace's face tightened. "You can't go back to the shop. Or to your apartment. Reporters are crawling all over the place."

"Storm can get the things I need." She took a shaky breath. Her heart felt as though it was thundering in her ears. "I made promises and I've got to keep them."

"Fine. Storm can bring your things to my house. You can work there."

Even though Trace's voice was a growl of angry frustration, hope edged back into Aislinn's soul.

"Let's get out of here," Miguel said, turning toward the car.

Voices drifted down the driveway. Sophie moved to Aislinn's side. "There are more reporters than before. One of them came around the house while you guys were inside."

Worry for Sophie flooded Aislinn. "Did they see you?"

Sophie nodded. "But I don't think he got a picture before one of the cops chased him off."

"He better not have," Storm muttered as they climbed into the car. "You two duck down. No use advertising that you were here."

Trace backed the unmarked car out of the drive, pissed when he saw how many reporters were waiting. The uniformed cop had called in backup units.

"Shit," Miguel said. "I guess we're going to see ourselves on the evening news." He turned to Storm. "Please tell me this trip was worth it."

"The perp probably took a souvenir with him."

Miguel grinned. "Hot damn. What'd he take?"

Storm cut a quick look at Aislinn before answering, "A crystal arrangement. Five stones in a holder that looks like a dragon."

Miguel's eyes swung to Aislinn. "From the store you work in?"

Aislinn nodded. "Yes."

Sophie slipped an arm around Aislinn's shoulders. "Could you feel the killer at all?"

"No," Aislinn whispered. "Just Patrick."

Sophie shivered. "It creeps me out that whoever killed Patrick took something you made. Maybe it's the same guy who kidnapped the Morrison kid and now he wants revenge."

Trace's hands tightened on the steering wheel at the mention of the Morrison kidnapping. "Not likely," he growled.

Sophie opened her mouth to say something, but Aislinn nudged her and said, "Only Storm."

"Only Storm what?" Miguel asked, but Sophie refused to say anything more until they were back at her apartment building and Trace had driven away with Aislinn.

"Okay, what gives?" Storm asked as the three of them stood next to one of the department's unmarked cars.

Sophie clasped her hands nervously in front of her. She shot a look at Miguel before telling Storm, "Maybe I can give you a call later."

Miguel took Sophie's hands in his. "Hey look, I know things got off to a strange start, but I'm trying to be open-minded about all of this. Don't hold anything back. It may be important."

"It's about the Morrison kidnapping," Sophie said.

Miguel shrugged. "Okay. That's not a hot button of mine. I'm just glad the kid is back home."

"Patrick didn't really find the kid. Aislinn did."

Silence greeted Sophie's pronouncement.

"Did Aislinn tell you that?" Miguel asked, his voice sharp.

Sophie stiffened. "If you're thinking she's crazy and just after the attention, then you're wrong. That's the last thing she wants!"

Miguel threw up his hands in defense. "Hey, hold on. I'm just trying to understand."

"Sorry," Sophie said on a sigh. "I didn't like Patrick. That's no secret. I guess he was good at some things. But he used Aislinn."

"Used her how?" Miguel asked, very glad that Trace wasn't here to hear this.

"There are things she can do that other people can't. Patrick could never have found that missing boy. When I cornered Aislinn about it, she admitted that she'd helped him. The parents gave Patrick a baseball glove that belonged to Thad and Patrick brought it to Aislinn." Sophie took a deep breath. "Aislinn can't find just anyone. It has to be someone who's frightened and wants to be found."

Storm's eyebrows were drawn together. "So Aislinn located the child, but Patrick is the one who told the parents and got the credit. Then later that night, Patrick gets murdered at just about the same time Aislinn is arriving at his house, and the murderer then takes something of Patrick's that Aislinn made." She shook her head. "I don't like the way this feels."

Miguel exhaled loudly. "You got that right. It might be a good thing she's on ice over at Trace's house."

Chapter Four

ဏ

Aislinn couldn't resist a peek at Trace as he brought the car to a halt in his driveway. Her pulse raced as she remembered the wild coupling that had taken place when he brought her home last night.

He hadn't said anything since leaving the others at Sophie's apartment. And yet the heat of his body and the erection that was pressed against the front of his jeans reassured Aislinn as no words could have.

"Let's go," he growled, not waiting for Aislinn to comply, but pulling her along with him as he left the car and walked to the front door. He pushed her inside, stopping just long enough to deactivate his alarm before pressing her against the wall and then covered her lips with his. She whimpered as his tongue thrust into her mouth and stroked aggressively against hers.

Home. It felt like coming home.

Her arms slipped around his waist. Her body softened and cuddled his, needing his touch, needing the heat of him to warm her.

Trace groaned and pulled away. His face was tight. "I can't stay long, but I can't leave without getting inside you."

His shirt fell just inside the doorway. His shoes and the rest of his clothing were an obvious trail to the bedroom. "Christ, you drive me crazy," Trace said as he removed Aislinn's clothing before pushing her onto the bed and latching onto a pale pink nipple. Her whimper sent more blood rushing to his already engorged penis. "You like this, don't you," he said, moving to the other breast. When she didn't answer immediately, he punished her with a sharp bite.

Aislinn arched upward. "Yes," she whispered, thrashing underneath him as he alternated between sucking and biting.

The small golden triangle of her pubic hair was a beacon trying to draw Trace's attention to where her cunt was swollen and wet. His. It reverberated over and over in his mind with the fast beat of his heart. She was his.

He wanted to roll her over onto her hands and knees and mount her. He wanted to push her down and make her wrap her hot little mouth around his cock. He wanted to crawl into her skin and know every inch of her. He wanted to consume her, possess her, own her completely.

It had never been like this before. But he couldn't stop the feelings racing through him. He didn't even want to try.

Aislinn felt as though her blood was on fire, as though every touch of his skin to hers bound them more tightly together. She needed him in a way that she'd never even dreamed was possible. She wanted to belong to him. Now and for always.

A shiver raced through her, causing her to arch into the wet suction of his mouth and rub her swollen clit against the firm muscles of his thigh. Fevered images flowed through her thoughts, things she'd never considered doing or having done to her.

Tentatively she slid her hand down and brushed it over the soft skin of his penis. Velvet over steel. She circled the huge organ with her fingers. Trace groaned against her nipple and pressed his cock into her hand. Emboldened, Aislinn rubbed her thumb against its silky tip, spreading the moisture weeping from his slit around the bulbous head.

Aislinn thrilled when Trace clenched his buttocks tightly and pumped into her hand, made helpless by her touch. But when she would have guided him into her, he growled and pulled away, capturing her hands and holding them at her sides as his mouth trailed wet kisses down her stomach.

He stopped just inches above her weeping cunt. "Spread your legs wider," he ordered, his voice tight and husky, his breath flowing over Aislinn's blood-swollen labia and clit.

When she didn't immediately obey, Trace lowered his head and ran his tongue along her slit. She jerked and he latched onto her clit, giving it a quick suck before letting it loose. "Open wider, baby. I want to see everything."

Aislinn trembled with sudden shyness, but she spread her legs and was rewarded by his praise. "You're so beautiful, baby. You're so swollen and wet that I could stay this way for days, looking at you—" he paused and moved in so that his soft mouth pressed against her sensitive skin, "—tasting you." His tongue stroked into her and she whimpered, unable to stop herself from arching so that his tongue could go deeper.

He thrust his tongue in and out, sending more blood pounding to her clit, causing her already flooded cunt to weep even harder. Trace groaned and pressed into her more tightly. His hands released hers and moved so that he held her thighs apart, pinning them to the bed so that he controlled every sensation.

Aislinn's hands flew to his head, her fingers buried themselves in his hair. Trace moved his attention to her swollen clit and she sobbed. Every stroke of his tongue sent a streak of lightning-sharp pleasure through her. "Please," she begged over and over again, not even sure what she was pleading for.

His face was strained, his breath short and his eyes dilated when he finally lifted his head. "That's right, baby, beg. Tell me what you need."

She tried to arch into him, to tell him with her body, but he held her firmly to the bed. "Do you want me to lick you? Suck you?" he asked.

Aislinn's womb clenched at the dark promise in his voice. "Yes," she pleaded.

"Then tell me that's what you want. Beg me to do it to you."

Liquid gushed from her cunt, coating her inner thighs. Trace turned his face, licking her quivering flesh before gripping her skin with his teeth and marking her with a hard sucking bite.

Aislinn's clit stood throbbing at attention, the delicate hood folded at its base. "Please, suck me," she whispered.

Trace lifted his head. His eyes blazed with masculine pride. Then, not taking his eyes off hers, he lowered his face and took her small organ into this mouth.

Aislinn jerked and sobbed. Pleasure pulsed from deep in her womb to the tips of her nipples as he sucked harder and faster. She thrashed against him, wanting to drive herself into his mouth, wanting him to swallow her whole. He growled and thrust his fingers into her cunt, shoving them in and out in time to his sucking, forcing her to give him everything, to cry out in a release that felt as though every cell, every nerve ending screamed in ecstasy. She was his.

Trace gripped his cock in his hand, trying to keep from spewing his seed. His head was buzzing. He felt high and Aislinn was his drug.

Her whimpers and screams had almost made him come on his sheets. He didn't think he could survive being outside her body much longer.

Her breath was still rushing in and out as she lay panting, shivering, legs spread, wet from his mouth and her own release. "Get on your hands and knees so I can mount you," he growled, almost afraid to touch her again, to take his hand off of his own cock.

She obeyed instantly, arching and crying out when he nipped the soft skin of her ass before nuzzling her cunt and sending his tongue along her slit. She spread her legs wider and Trace groaned at the sight of her swollen folds.

"What do you want?" he asked, moving so that his body covered hers.

"You," she whispered, pushing back against him.

There was no way he could draw it out any longer, no way he could tease the two of them higher. With a groan, Trace plunged his cock into her tight little channel.

Christ, he was never going to get enough of her.

Being inside her was pure heaven and pure hell. His hips bucked, driving his cock deeper into the tight fist of her sheath. He wanted it to last forever. He wanted to come right now. The conflicting needs only intensified the sensations whipping through his body.

Underneath him, Aislinn shifted, opening herself so that he drove deeper into her body on the next stroke.

Shards of white-hot demand raced down his spine and through his balls and cock.

It was more than he could stand.

He reached around and took Aislinn's clit between his fingers, squeezing it in time to his strokes. "Come for me, baby," Trace demanded as he pressed wet kisses against her neck. She cried out, fighting his demand until his fingers tightened on her sensitive nub and his teeth locked onto her shoulder.

Her tight walls clamped down on him as waves of heat washed over his cock. There was no way Trace could hold back any longer. He groaned, pumping his hips in a frantic fury as he came.

It had never been like this before, never. She made him want to dominate her, protect her, care for her.

Trace couldn't bring himself to separate from her. He knew he had to get back to work, but he didn't want to leave her body.

What was he going to do about this? About her?

He shifted so that they were on their sides, his cock still held in her tight depths. "How'd you get out of my house this morning?" he asked, not wanting to think about how it felt as though she belonged here, how every time he fucked her, his dick felt like it was home and didn't need to go anywhere else, ever.

Aislinn tensed at his question and Trace closed his eyes as her snug walls clamped down on him, making him pump involuntarily into her. Every cell in his body had screamed in satisfaction when he'd come, but that didn't mean he wasn't ready to do it all over again.

She traced a finger down his arm, hesitating so long that he didn't think she was going to answer. "Did Conner come by?" he prompted, still sure that his friend wouldn't actually give out the code, but not entirely sure that he wouldn't have freed Aislinn.

"No. I could tell which keys you touched. From there it was just trial and error."

Trace rubbed his cheek against her silky hair. Damn, he was getting too comfortable if he hadn't noticed his alarm keys getting worn. Yeah, it might take more math and more effort than your basic criminal was willing to put out, but noticing which keys were faded and then using multiple number combinations wasn't exactly complicated. He'd have to get the alarm company out to replace the keys.

"Can I trust you to stay here when I go back to work?" he asked. When she didn't immediately agree, Trace added, "I can't concentrate on who killed your friend if I have to spend my time worrying that some reporter is going to get a hold of you and give the killer something to be afraid about."

"For today, I'll stay. I can't promise past that."

Trace stroked her breast, pinching and tugging first one nipple and then the other before sliding his hand over her soft stomach and cupping her mound. When Aislinn shuddered and pressed even more tightly against him, he smiled, confident that he could convince her to stay.

* * * * *

"How'd the press conference go?" Miguel asked Conner when he and Storm got back to the bullpen.

"Fucking nuts. It was a free-for-all. Even the Captain almost lost his cool. Some nutso psychic named Madame Ava stood up and claimed she'd done a tarot card reading for Dean and warned him that she saw danger. Not only that, but she claims someone else is going to die. Jesus, where do these people come from? You think danger and death is hard to find? Just get in your car. Or go downtown after hours."

Miguel snorted with laughter. Storm frowned but didn't say anything.

"Dylan check in yet?" Miguel asked.

"Yeah. No luck with any of Dean's neighbors. He's on the way to the Morrison house right now. But my guess is they won't give him jack shit. What about with you guys?"

Miguel looked to Storm and she was the one to fill Conner in on what they'd learned at Dean's place. "Do you have access to Aislinn's apartment?" Conner asked. "It'd help if we could get a picture of the crystal piece that she thinks is missing."

Storm frowned at the way he'd phrased his wording, but didn't call him on it. "Sure, I can get a key from Sophie. If she doesn't know where Aislinn keeps her sketches, then I can call Trace's place and ask her." She looked down at the book that she'd removed from Dean's house. "What about this, you want me to follow up, maybe see if Dean has been in contact with the author?"

Conner and Miguel exchanged a look. "Sure, go ahead," Conner answered, glancing at the book and only barely able to suppress a smile as he noted the title again. *Tales of a Psychic Investigator.*

Storm gritted her teeth but managed to sound calm when she said, "I'll head out then."

As soon as she left the room, Conner laughed. "Shit. That was close. Another second and I probably would have managed to piss her off." He shook his head. "You got a take on any of this?"

"Other than feeling like I stepped into an alternate reality and any minute now my head is going to start spinning around, shades of *The Exorcist*? No."

* * * * *

"You have five seconds to move before I arrest you for trespassing, obstructing justice and interfering with the duties of an officer," Storm said as she came to a halt near the back stairs leading to Aislinn's apartment over Inner Magick.

The man sprawled out gracefully on the stairs grinned and slowly stood. "There's no need to get nasty, Officer, though I can understand why the police department is a little touchy these days. Should I assume the rumors are correct and Aislinn Windbourne is involved in the Patrick Dean murder? Or is the police department looking for a psychic to help them solve the case?"

Between the macho homicide cops and this guy, it took a lot of effort for Storm to rein in her temper. Cocky men set her teeth on edge. "And you are?"

"David Colvin."

"The *Channel 6* reporter?"

"I see my fame precedes me. Good. It saves so much time. You can understand now why it wouldn't be in the best interests of the police department to haul me off in handcuffs. Freedom of the press and so on."

Storm frowned at his arrogant grin, at the way his eyes danced. He was enjoying this and she'd love to end his little party. But not without the Captain's say-so. Shit, why did all the nice-looking guys have to be macho assholes or slippery scum, like David Colvin? Yeah, she knew who he was. She'd made a point of reading all the newspapers and watching as many of the news reports as possible before she'd made her pitch to the Captain and gotten the temporary transfer to work on the Dean case.

David Colvin might work for a respectable news organization, but he had the soul of a tabloid exploiter. His lead-ins had been the most inflammatory so far and he'd been the one to scoop Patrick Dean's connection to the Morrison kidnapping case.

"Freedom of the press doesn't mean freedom to trespass or interfere with a police investigation," Storm said, stepping forward and hoping that he wasn't going to push the issue.

Colvin waved a hand in the space between the building and his body. "By all means, please proceed." Storm gritted her teeth and climbed the stairs, grateful that she could squeeze past him without touching him.

Once inside Aislinn's apartment she paused in order to look around. She'd never been upstairs before. Storm gave a self-conscious laugh. In some ways she was as bad as the homicide cops. She'd expected to find a fortune-teller's den complete with beads hanging from the doorways and occult symbols on the walls. Instead she found a small, neat, uncluttered apartment.

The cop in her couldn't keep from looking around and trying to get a better sense of who Aislinn was. It was a risk defending Aislinn and taking what she'd said at the murder scene as absolute truth, but it wasn't a huge risk, especially for a cop who wasn't aiming for a detective's shield.

Storm was a beat cop and probably would be for the rest of her career. It suited her. So if word got around that she hung out with and believed in psychics, it probably wouldn't impact her work with the department—at least not too much. But it was still better to be safe than sorry.

Most of what she knew about Aislinn, she knew because of Sophie. Yeah, Sophie could sometimes go over the deep end and totally immerse herself when she got interested in a subject—like this thing with crystals—but Sophie was intelligent and analytical, so she wasn't an easy mark for a con artist.

Storm had to smile and admit that Aislinn would probably have made a good con artist. Damn if she hadn't done something to Trace! That alone was worth putting up with the egos in homicide. No way would she have ever guessed that Trace would fall and fall hard for someone who was so delicate and sensitive that she reminded Storm of an elf or a fairy.

Shaking off her amusement, Storm wandered through the apartment, just getting a feel for the place. She grimaced, aware that she was in fact trying to "open herself" to the vibes. Then she had to grin. Maybe she'd been hanging around with Sophie too much lately. Maybe this New Age stuff was starting to sink in a little too deeply.

But then again, all the best cops had something besides years of experience. They had instincts, gut feels, which Storm theorized was part survival instinct and part something else, something extrasensory.

There were only three rooms in the apartment, four if you counted the tiny closet of a bathroom. The kitchen was clean and clear of clutter, the sink empty of dishes. Aislinn had plants lined up along the windowsill underneath a small crystal arrangement.

Crystals sparkled in the muted light, holding Storm's attention momentarily and filling her with a sense of being safe, protected. And yet there was a haunting loneliness underneath. For a split second a flute's melody whispered across her consciousness in a distant, sad song, but disappeared when she blinked and looked away from the crystals.

"I am really losing it now," Storm said, hoping that the sound of her own voice would dispel the otherworld eeriness that still hovered around her.

She moved to Aislinn's bedroom. A similar crystal arrangement hung from the window above the bed, but Storm was careful not to look at it. "Chicken," she muttered, moving to the worktable where Sophie said that Aislinn kept her designs.

Out of curiosity Storm flipped though the papers on the table. The crystal arrangements were in varying degrees of completion. Some appeared simple, others more complex. But what caught Storm's attention were the notations scribbled in various places on each design. The script was like nothing she'd ever seen, and yet it was clearly a written language and not a collection of symbols.

She bent and opened the filing cabinet next to the workbench. The design that Aislinn had done for Patrick Dean was where it was supposed to be. There were no notations on it other than Dean's name, the date it was delivered and the source of the crystals that had gone into its making.

Storm flipped through the rest of the files in the drawer. None of the finished designs had the strange script on them.

It was a mystery that had Storm's attention. Her own "extra senses" hummed every time she looked at the script.

She knew that she didn't really have any business investigating further, but she couldn't stop herself from looking around the office for a copy machine so that she could take a sample of the script with her.

Not finding a copier, she took her cop's notebook out, but gave up in less than a minute. The script was too intricate for her to duplicate.

"Damn." She put the notebook back in her pocket and made a quick pass through the desk. No tracing paper either. "Guess I'll have to find the answer the old-fashioned way, by asking," Storm muttered as she put the Dean folder under her arm and checked to make sure that there was nothing showing that could feed the media frenzy.

She took one more look around the bedroom, this time forgetting to avoid the crystal hanging in front of the window. Once again it caught her attention, trapping her.

Though the arrangement looked the same as the one in the kitchen, the feelings were stronger in the bedroom. Storm forced herself to focus more intently on the crystal, to "hear it resonate" as Sophie liked to say.

Safety. That's what Storm got when she didn't fight the skepticism and denial. The crystal arrangement was there to ward against danger. But it seemed to amplify the other, too, the sense of loneliness and isolation.

Despite her open mind, Storm's heart beat a little faster as the melancholy, distant song of a flute whispered through her consciousness. *Okay, this is getting a little creepy.*

She couldn't stop the shiver that washed over her. Aislinn's father was a famous musician. A flute player.

Remembering the conversation that Conner and Aislinn had at the bar about her father's music, Storm wondered if maybe a CD was playing somewhere in the apartment. But as soon as she tried to pinpoint where the music was coming from, it was gone, along with the other sensations.

"This is so creepy," Storm said, more than ready to get back to the station. But her curiosity was piqued about Aislinn's father.

She found the music that Aislinn had mentioned, but there was no picture of the band on any of the six CDs. In fact, after Storm did another hasty tour around the apartment, she knew that there were no personal pictures anywhere. No awards. No anything, other than the drawings, that provided a clue as to Aislinn's life.

That made the cop in Storm extremely nervous.

She liked Aislinn, but the lack of personal memorabilia bothered Storm on a profound level. Only people with something to hide were so thorough in getting rid of everything from their past.

As far as she could tell, the only thing that tied Aislinn to anyone were the CDs. Storm frowned. Who was to say that Jessie Wolf was Aislinn's father? She didn't have his last name.

Storm didn't like where this was going. But she was a cop and there was no way that she could just look the other way. Maybe it was time to do a background check on Aislinn.

She thought about the drawings with the strange script. The language might hold a clue to her origins.

Damn, she hated this. Aislinn was Sophie's friend, but when it came to police work, friendships couldn't matter.

Storm retrieved the drawings, telling herself that she could justify taking them since Aislinn had said that she needed to finish some crystal work for her clients and there was no way she could come to her apartment and get them herself.

It was a stretch. Storm had thought Aislinn was talking about actual crystals and tools, but at least this gave her a chance to find out more. And it wasn't as though she was looking for admissible evidence.

Storm grimaced, for the first time thinking that maybe she shouldn't have asked the Captain to let her on this case. But it didn't stop her from checking the files under her arm in order to make sure that there was no hint of what they contained before she left the apartment.

She wasn't surprised to find the reporter—Colvin—lounging against the railing in a position that would force her to pass within inches of him. She tightened her grip on the files. If he forced her to drop them, then she was going to haul him in—media feeding frenzy or not.

* * * * *

Trace heard his cell phone ringing somewhere in the hallway, probably where his pants lay near the front door. The image made him grin.

Since his number wasn't common knowledge he didn't need too many guesses to figure that it was work-related. Damn. He could stay like this, cuddled up to Aislinn with his cock snugged into her tight little pussy all day. He grunted and pulled away, hating the sensation of being outside her body.

"Dilessio," he said after he got to the end of the hallway and retrieved the phone.

"I take it that you're still interrogating Aislinn." Conner's mocking voice had Trace grimacing. If he wasn't careful he was going to be the butt of a lot of jokes.

"Just about to leave. Anything new?"

"Yeah, the Captain wants you to bring her to the station."

"What!"

"Yeah, I knew you weren't going to like it." There was a long pause on the other end of the line before Conner added, "There's more. You want it now, or when you get here?"

"Spit it out."

"Dylan's ready to bring the Morrisons in. By the time he called to set up an appointment they were willing to talk—as long as the psychic from Inner Magick was present. Shocked the shit out of Dylan."

"Don't drag this out, what does it have to do with Aislinn?"

"The Morrisons think the psychic at Inner Magick is the one who located their son and they want to meet said person—in exchange for all the details of their meet with Dean. They have us and they know it. The last thing the department needs is for people to think we're harassing them."

"Christ, these people want to be in the spotlight."

"Yeah, that's what I would have thought, too. But some new information has come in. So when Dylan called, the Captain agreed, as long as the Morrisons were willing to come to the station."

Fury settled in Trace's gut. "What new information?"

"Look, just bring her in. We can settle it here. See you in a few."

Trace snapped the cell phone closed, pissed at Conner for dodging the question and hanging up. Fuck, this whole case was spinning out of control. He felt like his head was going to explode. He settled for storming back to the bedroom and hovering over Aislinn as he said, "The Morrisons want to see you."

The fact that she paled at the comment didn't help to calm him down. "Tell me what you have to do with them."

Aislinn slowly sat up. It brought her face only inches from his. "You won't believe me."

Trace closed his eyes briefly. Christ, he was pissed. He wanted to be pissed at her, too, for being involved in this mess. But the only thing he could think about was maybe taking his hand to her backside and pounding her sweet little ass while she writhed on his lap, and then fucking her until she swore she'd never so much as say the word psychic, much less have anything to do with anyone claiming to be one.

"Tell me."

"I never met them. Patrick did. He brought something that belonged to their son over to Inner Magick and I helped him locate Thad. But they weren't supposed to know. Patrick promised that he was the only one who'd know that I had anything to do with it."

Trace opened his mouth, not even sure what was going to come out. But before he could utter a word he saw Aislinn draw into herself just as she had before leaving him at the bar. It was there in her eyes, if he wasn't very careful about what he said, then she would walk away again. This time for good.

His heart grabbed his throat and clamped down hard, choking off the words until all he could manage was, "You'd better get dressed."

* * * * *

"Thank you for coming down to the station," Captain Ellis said, dropping back into the seat behind his desk as the Morrisons took opposite chairs.

Conner bit the inside of his mouth to keep from snorting at the Captain's polite handling of the Morrisons. Better the Captain than him. He still didn't buy any of this.

Though Conner had helped look for the Morrisons' kid, and seen their news conferences on TV, this was the first up close and personal look at them. The cop in him took their measure.

Ordinary. That's what came to mind.

The husband was middle-manager plump with too many days behind a desk and too few outside in the sun. The wife was office-worker-styled, glue-on nails, heavy on the hair spray, and already frowning.

Captain Ellis headed off trouble by saying, "One of our detectives is on his way in with the psychic."

Conner grinned, catching Miguel's quick look down and Dylan's rolled eyes. You had to hand it to the Captain, he could bullshit without blinking.

"Why don't we get started, from the events leading up to the kidnapping of your son through his rescue and any contact you had with Patrick Dean afterward," the Captain suggested.

Mrs. Morrison continued to frown but nodded to her husband as if he needed her permission to go ahead. He cleared his throat nervously and said, "I'll try to be brief since you're already aware of a lot of the details. Our son was kidnapped on Saturday. He'd been at the neighborhood park playing baseball with his friends, something he does most weekends. Usually he would have gone home with one of his friends or they would have come home with him, but we were going out of town for dinner with my brother-in-law, so he headed home on his own and was kidnapped. All he can remember is seeing an old van and noticing that the sliding door was open. The best guess from your detectives is that the kidnapper used something like chloroform to knock Thad out so he could be pulled into the van without anyone noticing. At least, the assumption is that the kidnapper used the van. No one came forward to identify it. As far as I know that's still the case." He paused and looked around for confirmation. The Captain nodded and Mr. Morrison continued telling what he knew.

"When Thad woke up he was being held in a room that had bars over the window and a slot cut out of the door so that meals could be slipped through. There was a bucket with water and a bucket for going to the bathroom, along with a mattress on the floor and a collection of comic books. When we went to the house with Patrick, we found Thad in that same room. He told us that he never left it, and he never saw either of the two men he'd heard arguing in the house."

Conner leaned forward at the mention of two men. Somehow the investigators on the Morrison case had managed to keep that fact under wraps. It hadn't made the rounds yet. Dylan shot him an easy-to-read look since they were both on the same page—the kidnapper and Patrick Dean arguing about how this publicity stunt was going to go down. But when Dylan opened his mouth, probably to follow up on that theme, the Captain cleared his throat in warning and asked, "Did Dean see the room where your son was being held?"

Mr. Morrison shook his head. "No. At least, I don't think so." He looked to his wife. Her brows drew together. "No. He was in another part of the house. I was the one who found Thad. Patrick left right after that. He didn't want to be around when the police got to the house. He knew that the reporters would be right behind them."

The Captain nodded as though that made perfect sense. Conner shot Dylan a look and grimaced. What bullshit.

"Did you see Patrick Dean again after you recovered your son?" the Captain asked.

"No," Mr. Morrison answered. "We talked by phone. That's the only contact we had."

"Did you know Dean before the kidnapping?" Captain Ellis asked.

"No," Mr. Morrison answered.

Mrs. Morrison straightened in her chair. "My husband and I are active members in our church. Under normal circumstances we wouldn't have had anything to do with someone like Patrick. But we were desperate. That's the only reason we contacted Patrick." She exchanged a glance with her husband before adding, "But we don't believe that Patrick was the one who located our son."

Conner couldn't remain quiet any longer. "Why is that?"

Mr. Morrison answered, "Patrick said that he needed something that belonged to our son, something that was important to Thad. We took Thad's baseball glove with us when we went to Patrick's house."

Mrs. Morrison leaned forward. "Quite frankly, we expected Patrick to put on a show with a lot of mumbo jumbo. We were very surprised when he wanted us to leave the glove and go home. When we didn't want to do that, he began acting...odd." Her eyebrows drew together again. "Anxious, perhaps. He insisted that he could help us get our son back, but that he couldn't get a 'reading' with us there. We left the glove, but instead of going home we parked down the street from Patrick's house. We told Patrick that if he needed to reach us immediately he should call my cell number."

"A few minutes after he thought we were gone, he left and we followed him to Inner Magick. He was only in that shop for about thirty minutes. When he came out and got in his car, he called us immediately and said that he thought he knew where to look for Thad. We agreed to a meeting place and you know the rest of the story."

"So Patrick Dean knew the exact address of the house?" Captain Ellis asked.

"No," Mr. Morrison said. "He described what Thad could see through the window. We drove around for an hour before finding the house."

The Captain steepled his fingers. "There are several dozen psychics practicing in this area. Why did you choose Patrick Dean?"

The Morrisons exchanged glances. Mrs. Morrison nodded slightly. Her husband answered, "One of the reporters suggested we contact him. It was after we went on television to plead for Thad's return. We didn't have anything to lose, except our pride, if all she was after was a story. That seemed like a small price to pay if we might get Thad back."

Mrs. Morrison gave the Captain a direct look. "We've answered your questions. Now we'd like to see the psychic from Inner Magick."

The Captain reached over and pushed a button on his desk intercom. "Trace here?"

A woman's voice answered, "Not yet."

"Call his cell and see how close he is."

"Will do."

The Captain pulled his hand back. "Which reporter directed you to Patrick Dean?"

The Morrisons exchanged looks again. It was the wife who answered, "Khemirra Reis. She's a freelance reporter."

Conner frowned. The name didn't ring any bells. Thanks to the torture of the press conference that the Captain had insisted he be a part of, Conner thought he would know who the "enemy" players were.

Captain Ellis didn't indicate one way or another whether the name meant anything to him. He nodded in the direction of the other policemen in the room and said, "Maybe the other detectives have some questions."

Dylan leaned forward immediately and said, "You said that your son was coming home from playing baseball when he was kidnapped. Is that correct?"

The Morrisons nodded in unison. Dylan continued smoothly, "And yet you took Thad's baseball glove with you when you went to meet Dean. Wouldn't your son have had his glove with him?"

Mrs. Morrison's reaction was an immediate stiffening of her back and tightening of her lips. Mr. Morrison twitched and hurried to say, "He'd just gotten a new glove for his birthday. That's the glove he had with him."

Conner wasn't surprised that they had the story worked out. He decided to play the believing cop to Dylan's skeptical one. His gut told him that the husband was the weak link in this family chain. He focused a friendly smile on Mr. Morrison. "It was probably a lucky break for you that he had the new glove with him. I assume that the old glove held a lot of value for your son. I imagine Dean said that having something like that would make it easier to find Thad."

Mr. Morrison's shoulders sagged in relief. "Yes. I think that's why we were able to get Thad back so quickly."

Conner smiled another friendly smile. "I'm sure the detectives handling your case already asked you this, but for the record, are you convinced that Patrick Dean didn't have anything to do with your son's kidnapping?"

Rather than be offended by the question, Mr. Morrison actually seemed relieved to have it out in the open. He looked over at his wife before answering. "I'll admit that it crossed my mind. As my wife mentioned, we're active in our church and this experience is outside of our religious beliefs, that's part of why we wanted to come down here. We want...we need to meet whoever Patrick asked to help find Thad. We need to find a way to reconcile this with our beliefs."

The intercom buzzed and a woman's voice said, "Captain, Trace just got here."

The Captain reached over and pushed a button down. "Thanks, Kathy. Tell him to hold for a few minutes." He released the button and said to the Morrisons, "Do you have your son's glove with you?"

Mrs. Morrison's lips pursed together for a second before answering, "Yes. I think it's still in the car, under the passenger's seat."

"Would you mind if one of the detectives goes out and gets it?"

"Of course not," she answered.

The Captain shot Dylan a look. "You followed them in?" Dylan nodded. "Good, then you can go get the glove." As Dylan left the room Captain Ellis picked up the phone and made a call. "Bell, you still coaching little league?... Good. You still carrying around a sack of gloves?... Good. Get them up to interrogation. Kathy'll tell you which room." He put the phone down and compressed the button on his intercom. "Find us an interrogation room. Send Bell there when he comes in. Tell him to lay out the gloves on the table, then make himself scarce. He wants to hang behind the glass with me and observe, fine, otherwise I'll take responsibility for getting the gloves back to him. When Dylan gets back inside, send him up. Tell him the same thing. Then buzz Trace and tell him which room we're going to be in. But tell him to hold off coming up with the psychic until he gets the word."

Conner could barely suppress a grin. *Damn, the Captain was really working it!* He looked over to see what the Morrisons were making of this turn of events. The wife had her usual sour expression, the husband seemed like he might be admiring the Captain's style, too.

The Captain turned back to the Morrisons. "We'll ask the psychic to pick out Thad's glove before introducing you to her," he said with a straight face that had Conner forcing down a laugh. "Obviously you've both been through an extremely difficult time. We don't want to add to your burden by needlessly involving you in this murder case if there's no apparent connection."

When the Morrisons nodded their heads in agreement, Captain Ellis smiled and rose from his chair. "Let's head to interrogation."

Chapter Five

The police station was a fascinating place. Though Aislinn had never been in one before, thanks to Sophie's taste in television shows, the hustle and bustle, the constant sound of telephones ringing, the cubicles with their desks covered in paperwork and used coffee cups all seemed so familiar.

She sat in the chair next to Trace's workstation while he spoke to someone on his cellular. He was frowning slightly, but his grip on her hand hadn't tightened. His thumb continued to sweep feather-soft across her knuckles, offering comfort and reassurance.

Aislinn wondered if he was even aware of what he was doing. She prayed that the simple gesture came from his heart.

They hadn't spoken since leaving his home. The silence made her want to retreat behind her protective walls. That was how she'd survived when she lived among her mother's people. But to cut herself off from Trace would hurt too much. To be without his touch would be like living without the sun.

She took a shaky breath. Surely this was the beginning of the heartbond.

Trace closed his cellular phone and slipped it into his pocket before turning to her. "There're ready for us." His voice was a low unhappy growl, but the grip on her hand was secure and comforting. "Let's go," he said as he rose from his chair and helped Aislinn to her feet.

She could feel the interest of the other detectives as Trace guided her toward the door. Several snickered as they passed and Trace shifted his grip to her elbow.

His tension grew as they made their way upstairs. Miguel stood midway down the hall in front of a closed door. "The Captain wants me to take her in," he told Trace.

The fingers on Aislinn's elbow tightened. "What's going on?" Trace asked.

Miguel shifted uncomfortably. "The Captain's waiting, I need to take her from here."

Trace nodded his head toward the closed door. "He in there with the Morrisons?'

"No." Unhappiness flickered across Miguel's face. "Look, let's just get this over with."

The door across from where they stood opened. A uniformed officer led a handcuffed man out of the room. Two other men followed. From where she stood, Aislinn could see a table bolted to the floor and recognized it as an interrogation room.

Her heart sounded loud in her ears. Scenes from Sophie's police shows flashed through her mind, scenes where detectives tried to lure suspects into confessing their crimes. She shivered and looked to Trace. His frown was fierce. "I don't want her going in there without backup."

A brief smile lightened Miguel's expression. "I'll be with her." He shrugged. "Maybe the Captain will let you come in later."

"Are you going to ask me more questions?" Aislinn asked.

Miguel shifted nervously which did nothing to calm Aislinn's increasing anxiety. "This is mainly for the Morrisons' benefit. It's nothing to be worried about. Just do what you need to do and it'll be okay." He cut a look to Trace. "I need to get her inside now, before the Captain gets pissed and wonders what the delay is about."

Trace nodded and dropped his hand from Aislinn's elbow. For a second the loss of contact made her feel as though she'd been plunged into an icy pit. But before she could become truly afraid, he leaned forward and brushed his lips against hers. "It'll be okay, baby. I'll be watching. As soon as we're done here, I'll take you home."

His reassurance gave her the courage to enter the interrogation room and face the task that she knew awaited as soon as she saw all the baseball gloves spread out on the table and overflowing onto the chairs.

"The Morrisons brought Thad's glove," Miguel said as he closed the door and took a stance in front of it.

Aislinn looked around the room and guessed which wall held the one-way glass. "They're watching?" she asked, once again grateful for Sophie's choice of television shows. In so many ways this world was far more complex than Elven-space.

Miguel shrugged but didn't answer. Aislinn walked over to stand in front of the table. Her eyes were immediately drawn to Thad's glove. It looked no different than many of the other gloves, but his signature-touch was a beacon that made it unmistakable to her.

She didn't want to select it, didn't want those watching to have proof of her ability. Yet what choice was there? If she didn't do this, then how would she get them to believe her if she found anything else that might aid them in catching Patrick's murderer?

Aislinn shivered. It violated no Elven law to use her magic in the human world. But there was always a risk in doing so. If she drew too much attention to herself, the elders might notice and rule that she must leave.

The thought kept her hand tethered to her side for a long moment. But ultimately her honor required her to take that risk. She reached over slowly and touched one of five gloves positioned on a chair. "This is the glove Patrick brought with him."

"Are you sure?"

"Yes," she said, letting her hand drop away from the glove as she turned to look at Miguel.

He shrugged. "They'll let us know what to do next."

She drew a shaky breath and waited. It took only a moment before Dylan came through the door and walked over to the glove she'd selected. Picking it up, he said, "Come on, the Morrisons are waiting for you in another room."

* * * * *

Trace slammed his fist against the wall as soon as the Morrisons left the observation room. "Son of a bitch, I hate this stuff!"

Conner grunted. "Don't we all."

Captain Ellis continued to stand in front of the one-way mirror. On the other side Dylan entered the room and picked up the glove. "That wasn't a lucky guess," he said. "The Morrison kid's glove looked like at least ten of the other gloves, more if she didn't remember who endorsed it." He turned to Trace. "My gut is starting to churn harder on this one. Trace, as soon as the psychic gets done talking to the Morrisons, get her out of here. Conner, hunt down that reporter who put the Morrisons onto Dean."

* * * * *

Aislinn felt completely drained by her meeting with the Morrisons. They'd wanted some kind of closure, some kind of understanding how she'd been able to do what she'd done. She wasn't sure that meeting her had provided that for them. Some things required true belief. Magic was one of them.

The door to the interrogation room opened and Trace walked in. Aislinn stood and hurried to him, wanting the comfort of his arms. But the tight expression on his face kept her from pressing against his body. Her heart stilled in her chest like a roller coaster car ready to plunge downward.

Christ, he wanted her. Even right now with the Captain probably watching from the other side, Trace wanted to crush her little body against his. He was hard as a rock and hurting.

"Can we leave now?" Aislinn said, her voice so soft and feminine that it felt like a hand was wrapped around his cock, stroking him.

Trace gritted his teeth and tried to distance himself. He couldn't.

Fuck! How had this happened?

The stunt with the glove should have killed off this attraction. But all he wanted to do was get her back to his house and pound into her.

"Yeah, let's go." He stepped back so that she could precede him through the door, then gritted his teeth as a cloud of silky blonde hair brushed against his arm when she passed. He closed his eyes briefly and tried to rein in the erotic images that assailed him. What was he going to do about this? About her?

Trace took her arm and guided her out of the station and back to his car. A reporter yelled a question but Trace ignored it, hoping it was directed at someone else. The question came again, followed by a chorus of other voices. He looked up this time and started cursing. Son of a bitch, it seemed like the place was crawling with reporters. How were they supposed to get any work done with a rabid audience like this?

He got Aislinn into the car then climbed in after her and slammed the door. She reached over and laid a soft hand on his arm. For a second he could only stare at it.

"If you'd rather take me to Sophie's, I understand," she whispered.

Trace swung his attention to her face and was lost. The wariness he saw there pierced him like a physical wound. She was always so ready to run from him.

In a heartbeat, anger transformed into something else, something equally primitive—possessiveness. She was his and it was time she knew it. He pulled her to him and settled his mouth over hers in a kiss that didn't ask, but demanded.

Aislinn's body responded even as her mind tried to hold back, unsure of his mood, of the anger that resonated from him. But it was impossible to deny Trace when all she wanted to do was melt into him.

With a whimper she pressed herself against him. The deep rumble of a satisfied growl vibrated through his chest, massaging her sensitive nipples. His tongue thrust against hers, then retreated. When she followed with her own he held it hostage in the wet heat of his mouth before releasing it and once again stroking into her. She was panting by the time he ended the kiss.

Trace held her so that their faces were only inches apart. "No matter how mad I get about this psychic shit, I'll never take it out on you," he said, punctuating his statement with another brief fierce kiss. "So stop trying to run away from me. Understand?" Aislinn nodded. "Good."

He started the car then took her hand in his, holding it in his lap, against his hard need. By the time Aislinn entered his home, her heart was pounding, her pulse racing. Did she dare?

She shivered at the sound of the door closing behind them and turned back to him before she lost her nerve. "I need you," she whispered, curling her hands around the leather of his belt.

His face tightened instantly as eyelids lowered, though not enough to cover the flame of arousal that her words had caused. "Show me," he ordered and the rough timbre of his voice helped her find the courage to proceed.

Aislinn licked her lips and felt the quick jump of his cock against the front of his pants. Heat rushed to her face. Her body pulsed with remembered pleasure. When he'd made love to her with his mouth and tongue it had been beyond anything that she could have imagined.

She wanted to give him that same pleasure. She wanted to draw it out as he'd drawn it out for her.

She undid his belt—slowly. Then pulled the zipper of his pants down, being sure that her fingers traced along the erection pressing against his jockeys.

When the zipper was down, she peeled back his pants and leaned over, nuzzling his still-concealed cock.

It twitched against her only seconds before Trace's fingers were wrapped in her hair, holding her against him. "Don't tease me, baby, unless you're willing to give me what I want," he growled.

Aislinn edged his jockeys lower, just far enough that the tip of his cock was exposed. Trace's washboard stomach tightened in response. She looked up to see his face.

A wave of lust mixed with feminine power rushed through her at the feral light in his eyes, at the way his lips were opened slightly with anticipation. "Do it," he ordered and because she wanted to, she did.

Aislinn brushed a soft kiss over the tip of his penis and was rewarded by his hiss of pleasure as his hips pumped upward. She swirled her tongue over the bulbous head then took it into her mouth, gently sucking.

Trace moaned and hunched over, tightening his hands in her hair before jerking away with a harsh, guttural sound. "Not here," he said, picking her up and quickly moving toward the bedroom.

As he walked he kicked off his shoes, but he didn't strip out of the rest of his clothing. When he got to the bedroom he fell onto the bed with Aislinn, then maneuvered onto his back before shoving his pants and jockeys down so that the full, engorged length of his cock was exposed.

Aislinn's heart pounded at the sight of it, at the need she read in his face. She took his penis in her hand and stroked up and down its length, enjoying the texture and fullness of it. Trace's hands went to her head, his fingers smoothing over her cheeks and lips before sliding into her hair. "Put your mouth on me, baby. Show me how much you like my cock."

She lowered her head but didn't give in immediately. Instead she let her warm breath move over him, then her tongue. She laved him from the tip to the base, tracing the heavy veins with her tongue then investigating the darkening head with its wet slit.

Trace arched and groaned beneath her. "Baby, you're killing me. Put me in your mouth. Take me in as far as you can."

Aislinn shivered at the need in his voice. She'd never imagined doing this to a man, but her own desire was amplified by his. She wanted to give him everything, to be what he needed.

She parted her lips, but only slightly, so that when he pushed upward, seeking the haven of her mouth, there was a brief resistance before the tip of him was in.

Trace groaned. The streaks of pleasure ripping through his dick were almost more than he could take.

She was making him crazy with her tight mouth and wet licks. He wasn't sure how much more of this he could stand before he grabbed her head and forced her to finish him.

Christ, she turned him on, brought out a primitive part of him that he managed to keep suppressed most of the time. His hands tightened in her hair and she began sucking him, tentatively at first, then with more demand as he began pumping in and out of her mouth.

"That's it, baby, show me how much you want me."

She answered by drawing him deeper into her mouth, into her throat, by swallowing. Trace closed his eyes, unable to stand the dual pleasure of watching and feeling what she was doing to him at the same time.

He was desperate.

Desperate to keep fucking her mouth.

Desperate to rip himself away and shove himself into her pussy.

Desperate to come.

But the sensations coursing through his cock and up his spine were so intense, so unbelievable that he couldn't think, couldn't decide how he wanted to spend himself.

Aislinn decided for him when her fingers slid down and cupped his balls, squeezing them in time to her sucking.

With a shout, Trace exploded in a mind-numbing, seemingly endless orgasm, only releasing his grip on Aislinn's hair when the last vestige of pleasure faded from his cock.

When Aislinn lifted her flushed, dazed face and licked her lips, some of the blood pounding in Trace's head rushed back to his cock. He pulled her alongside his body and pressed her back against the comforter.

"That was so good, baby," he whispered, his eyes staring deeply into hers, his face so close that the tips of their noses touched in a gentle caress. "Now I'm going to return the favor." He pushed aside her shirt and bra then began kissing her neck, her shoulders, the slopes of her breasts.

Aislinn closed her eyes and arched upward, trying to draw his attention to nipples that were hard and aching. She could feel him smile against her skin before moist lips moved slowly downward and a wet tongue circled her areola.

"Trace," she whispered, part demand, part need.

In response he licked and pressed soft wet kisses against her aching flesh. Then took her nipple deep into his mouth, sucking and pulling on it as though he wanted to swallow it. Aislinn arched upward and cried out, digging her hands into his hair to hold him against her breast, barely aware of his hand slipping along her side until he pulled her pants and underwear away from her heated flesh and took her clit between his fingers.

Trace left no room for resistance, even if she'd wanted to resist him. He circled and stroked her clit, then plunged his fingers into her and pumped in time to the deep hard sucks on her nipple. Fire raced through her, causing her toes to curl and her body to jerk. He responded by pressing more of his weight on her, holding her down in silent dominance. Against her hip he was rock-hard, the tip of him wet and dripping with his own excitement.

"Please, Trace," she whimpered.

He left her breast and rose above her, his face flushed and feral looking as he hovered over her and put the engorged tip of his penis against her wet, open slit. "Watch," he ordered, entering her by slow inches.

She watched, unable to take her eyes away from the place where their bodies joined. Instinctively, she tightened on him, increasing the sensation, the pleasure.

Above her Trace panted, closing his eyes briefly against the intensity, the furious need that was building. He wanted to slam in and out of her. He wanted to savor every slow inch.

"Touch your clit," he ordered, his voice harsh with need.

She slid her delicate fingers over the engorged knob and shuddered, tightening on him like a wet, silken vise. "That's it, baby, stroke yourself while I fuck you."

He began pumping, slowly at first, then with more force, mesmerized by the sight of his cock moving in and out of her, by the sight of Aislinn's fingers caressing and massaging her flushed, swollen clit.

When she cried out, arching and tightening on him in release, Trace couldn't hold back any longer. He closed the distance between their bodies and pumped furiously as blinding pleasure whipped down his spine and through his cock.

Even when the extreme pleasure had subsided, Trace didn't want to pull out of her, didn't want to leave the sweet haven of her cunt. Christ, what was he going to do about this? He didn't need to be psychic to know that his cock wasn't going to want anybody else for a long time, maybe ever. He buried his face in her hair and breathed her in.

He was in trouble. It had never been like this with any other woman—never. He'd come twice, hadn't even pulled his cock out of her and it was already filling with blood again, getting ready for a third time.

He lifted his face and looked into hers. Fuck, she was so delicate, so fragile.

Trace couldn't stop himself from leaning down and tracing his tongue along the seam of her lips. She parted them immediately and met his tongue with the tip of hers. "You're so sweet, baby," he whispered, resting more of his weight on her.

Aislinn whimpered and he had to close his eyes against the sight of her, against the almost immediate need to dominate that rose within him every time she made that soft, submissive sound. "Wrap you legs around my waist," he ordered.

She complied and his cock sunk deeper into her tight channel. "That's right, baby, we're going to take it slow and easy this time," he whispered as his lips returned to hers.

Aislinn shivered underneath him and Trace held himself still inside her. Christ, it was almost more than he could stand. He'd never had a woman react to him like she did. Hell, he'd never reacted to a woman like this. If it didn't feel so good, it would scare the shit out of him.

He touched her lips with his, stroked his tongue into her mouth in the same slow tempo that his cock moved in and out of her. Her fingers traced along his spine and Trace's buttocks clenched in reaction. She whimpered again and shifted, opening herself wider, and a rush of primitive satisfaction washed over Trace. "What do you want, baby?"

"You."

The heat of her seared his cock, the look in her face burned through Trace's control. She was open to him in every way, vulnerable, and it made him want to possess her, protect her.

His reality narrowed to just the two of them and he couldn't take his eyes off of hers. He held out as long as he could, keeping it slow and easy as she writhed underneath him, tightening her legs around his waist and whimpering, her face full of helpless need.

Fire ripped down Trace's spine, his balls pulled tight against his body, and his strokes quickened. "Come for me, baby," he panted, holding back until Aislinn sobbed and her orgasm washed over him.

Aislinn had never imagined it would be like this. Never imagined the wanting, the needing, the closeness. Her heart argued that she'd found the one made for her, that what she felt with Trace was the heartbond of her mother's people. But she didn't dare speak to Trace about it. Didn't dare ask him if he wanted more from her than this. She didn't want to ruin this moment when their bodies were so tightly merged that it felt as though they were one person. Slowly their breathing returned to normal. Aislinn braced herself, ready for him to ask about what had happened at the police station, how she'd been able to recognize the glove. Instead he grunted and pulled away, sitting up, but not leaving the bed.

"I've got to get back to work." He smoothed a hand over her stomach before tracing upward to her breasts, then her lips, and finally cupping her chin. "You'll stay put this time, right?"

"Yes."

Trace leaned over and kissed her. "Good. You like Italian food?"

"Yes."

"I'll bring some home with me. Help yourself to anything you find here." He kissed her again, this time more fiercely. "Don't go outside. Don't let anyone in."

"I need some of my things, so I can work."

Trace's hand dropped away from her face, leaving the place where he'd touched suddenly cold. Aislinn could see the withdrawal echoed in the coolness of his eyes. "Just don't let anyone in besides Sophie or one of the cops you know."

"Okay," she said, a shiver of pain wrapping around her heart. If he never accepted this part of her, how could they truly be heartbonded?

Maybe because she was neither fully human nor fully elf, there would be no heartbond for her. What if this was all she could expect in her father's world?

Trace rose from the bed and escaped to the bathroom. He let the hot water pound him while he tried to pull himself together. Shit, he was a mess. He was like some junkie, ready to rationalize, to look the other way, to avoid reality so he didn't have to give up his drug, his high— Aislinn.

It was like a cold slap every time he had to confront the psychic crap. Hell, he'd managed to avoid even thinking about what happened at the station. Instead he'd focused on getting her home, on getting her to agree to stay, on getting inside her sweet, wet channel.

Trace turned so that the water pummeled his face. A soft click warned him of Aislinn's presence, and then she was in the shower with him, gently taking the soap from his hands and smoothing it over his body. He groaned, but couldn't bring himself to stop her.

Aislinn immersed herself in the pleasure of simply stroking Trace's body, of smoothing soap-slick hands over his muscles and watching as the suds washed downward. If this was all she was to have, then she'd enjoy every moment of it.

Trace returned the favor, soaping his own hands and running them over her still-sensitive skin. She shivered when he got to her ears and traced the delicate butterfly earrings that covered Elven tips. Though the sensation was muted by the crystal-enhanced metal, her ears were an erogenous zone. Each stroke along them caused her nipples and cunt to tighten, to ache.

When Trace replaced his fingers with his lips and tongue, Aislinn couldn't stop the whimper of need that escaped. She pressed herself against him, her breath coming in short pants as his tongue outlined her ears then swirled delicately into the small canal before sucking the lobe into his mouth.

Trace pushed his thigh between her legs and lowered his hands to her hips, holding her tight. Aislinn whimpered again and started riding him, pressing her throbbing clit against his water-slick flesh.

The blood pounded in Trace's head and cock. Her response was an aphrodisiac. "Don't come on my leg, baby," he whispered, daring himself to give in to some of his darker fantasies. "I'll punish you if you do."

Aislinn stilled for a heartbeat. The desire to dominate radiated from Trace and was answered from deep within her by the need to submit. It was the same beguilement she'd felt when she first met him, the desire that made her want to be completely mastered by her mate.

She rubbed the warmed crystal of her earring over his lips, enticing him. When he stroked his tongue along the skin just below the delicate butterfly she jerked against him, pressing and rubbing her clit against his thigh in time to the wet lashes of his tongue.

A thrill shot through Trace at her reaction to his words. His cock throbbed. His balls were tight and heavy in anticipation.

She was close to coming. Trace freed one of his hands from Aislinn's hips and lifted it to her other ear, teasing the ultra-sensitive tip with his fingers.

The dual attack on her erogenous zone was more than Aislinn could stand. Unable to stop the frantic pumping of her body, she whimpered with each strike of her clit against his thigh, until finally she sobbed in release.

Trace lifted her higher against his body, fighting the urge to plunge into her when she wrapped her legs around him and pressed her hot little body fully against his. She was still shivering from orgasm as he pushed the shower door open, intent on getting her to the bedroom.

His mind raced with what he wanted to do to her, how he'd carry out his threat of punishment. But as soon as he stepped out of the bathroom he was assailed by the sound of ringing. Like a bad two-part melody, the telephone in his bedroom jarred against the chime of his cell.

Shit. It had to be urgent.

Chapter Six

ହ

"Why me?" Conner muttered as he dropped the receiver back into its cradle and stared morosely at the notes—or lack thereof—that he'd taken while talking to the reporter.

Miguel looked up from his desk. "Dead end? "

"Probably. She's willing to meet me—off the record."

Miguel snorted. "Serves you right for being the Captain's pet on this one. You didn't see him asking me to the press conference."

Conner ripped the top piece of paper off his notepad, crushed it into a ball, and tossed it at his partner. Miguel dodged it and Conner said, "If you're feeling left out, you can come with me and talk to the reporter."

Miguel laughed. "No can do. I've got an appointment with a psychic."

"What!"

Miguel shrugged. "It's not like we have any other hot leads right now. Might as well talk to some other psychics. Get their take on Dean. Right now we only have Aislinn's and the Morrisons'. They're all too close to the case. Maybe professional jealousy led to Dean's murder. Won't know until we ask around."

There was a long moment of silence. "Shit. Tell me you're not starting to buy into this stuff," Conner finally said.

"You've met Aislinn. You want to explain what happened up in interrogation with the glove?"

Conner shook his head. "Shit. If she's a con, she's a smooth one, and Trace is in trouble. Hell, we're all in trouble."

Miguel rose from his chair. "Yeah, the sooner we can get this case put away, the better."

* * * * *

By the time Conner got to the park, he felt edgy and pissed. This was a fucking waste of time.

He could already recite how this conversation with Khemirra Reis was going to go down.

Why'd you suggest that the Morrisons contact Patrick Dean?

I'm sorry, the First Amendment covers that information.

Yeah, I understand that. But maybe you know something that could help us solve the Dean murder. Since you sent the Morrisons that way and Dean ended up dead as a result, maybe you can overlook citing the First Amendment in the interest of some justice for the psychic.

I'm not responsible for Patrick Dean's death. I'm sorry he was murdered, but I can't share information with you.

Then she'd go on about reporters' integrity while Conner did a slow boil and only barely managed to keep from finding a reason to cuff her and take her downtown so she could hang out in a jail cell full of lowlifes. Maybe that would give her a change of attitude about bad guys and why she should protect them.

Conner rubbed his neck and tried to let some of the tension go as he wandered through the park entrance. There were a handful of women watching as small children tossed pieces of bread to a loud collection of ducks and geese. Other than that, the place was quiet, and despite his mood, Conner couldn't completely fight off the tranquil nature of the park.

Damn, he needed to get to the mountain cabin his folks had and just hang out for a while. No phones. No noise except for what belonged in the woods. It'd been too long. When this case was over he was going to take some time off, even if he had to go without female companionship. He'd never taken a woman to the cabin. The place was his private retreat, his den, unless other members of his family were crashing there, then it was just a hell of a good time.

Conner's mind skittered to Aislinn. Too bad Trace had already staked a claim on her. There was something about Aislinn that fired off some pretty vivid domination fantasies. He shook his head. Who was he kidding? He liked a little more fire, a little more fight, in his women. Trace had always gone for that, too, though he wasn't averse to fucking long-legged, big-boobed bimbos, either. Until now.

Conner grinned. From the looks of it Trace was walking around with an almost constant hard-on. Who'd have guessed that Trace would fall so hard for someone as soft and in need of protection as Aislinn? Christ, and she came with all that psychic bullshit, too. He shook his head.

It didn't matter how good a fuck the woman was, how hard she made his dick or how much he enjoyed her company, he was not getting involved with anyone who had anything to do with supernatural shit. No way.

The path opened up and Conner spotted the reporter he'd been ordered by the Captain to interview. He was several steps away when she rose from the bench and sent his blood roaring south.

Midnight hair surrounded a face that was both feminine and strong. Dark jeans and a dark top molded like a second skin to a body that was lithe and sleekly muscled. But it was the eyes that drew Conner's attention. Brown so light that they were almost amber. Wolf eyes, like he'd seen once when he was a day's hike away from the cabin.

His immediate instinct was to push her to her knees and mount her.

The amber eyes widened slightly, as did her nostrils, giving Conner the impression that she was scenting him. He moved in, too close to be polite, but he couldn't help himself. She moved back in a familiar dance that had nothing to do with personal space and everything to do with the press and retreat that came before mating.

"You must be Conner," she said in a voice that was slightly husky, a voice that ran the length of Conner's spine and curled around to cup his balls.

"And you're Khemirra."

She nodded and retreated further, to the other side of the bench. Conner wanted to follow, to stalk her around the park if he needed to—and not just to get the information he came for.

He indicated the bench. "You want to sit and talk or do this standing?"

A pink tongue darted along the seam of her lips, drawing Conner's attention to them. This time it was his nostrils that flared, him that wanted to scent her, to taste her. "I'd rather walk if that's okay with you," she said.

"Sure, fine."

She looked over her shoulder and Conner got the impression that she was watching for someone and it didn't have anything to do with him. He tested the waters. "Afraid of being seen talking to a cop?"

Khemirra's eyes jerked back to Conner, but she relaxed. The shift in stance seemed natural enough to him, but he couldn't be sure that it wasn't forced. "You wanted to talk about the Morrison kidnapping and the Dean murder," she said.

"Yeah, the Morrisons were good enough to come to the police department. They said you were the one who suggested they give Dean a call. Why was that?"

She pulled away, put several more inches between them and Conner found that he didn't like that. He grabbed her arm and pulled her close. Their bodies brushed against each other and her amber eyes widened, then narrowed. "It was just a suggestion. They were desperate and I wanted to help."

"Why Dean?" Conner growled. "There are plenty of other psychics you could have suggested."

She surprised Conner by furrowing her brow as though she was considering his question and thinking about answering it. He loosened his grip but didn't take his fingers from her arm.

Fuck, he could feel the heat radiating off her. His cock tightened at the image of sweat-slick bodies sliding against each other.

Conner grinned. Her cunt would probably burn him alive.

As if sensing the direction of his thoughts, Khemirra eased away again, this time stopping and turning slightly so that they could look at each other. Conner forced his mind back to the reason he was here. Yeah. He wanted to get this case put to bed. Then he wanted to bed this reporter.

Khemirra's brows were still furrowed as she said, "I ran into a couple of reporters at Starbucks. They were swapping stories about other kidnappings and how they'd ended. Everyone was worried about finding the child in time. Somehow the conversation rolled around to psychics, I think the reporter from *Channel 6* said that his mother was a big believer in psychics and maybe the Morrisons should see one. Another reporter chimed in and said he'd been on the crime beat when the cops had hauled in a couple of psychics for fraud. Someone else, I think it was the reporter from the *Times*, said he'd done a piece on a man named Patrick Dean who actually seemed to have some things going for him. Dean's was the only name that came up, I guess that's why I mentioned it to the Morrisons."

"Do you remember which *Times* reporter mentioned Dean?"

Khemirra shook her head. "I don't remember his name. He was older. Gray hair and bushy eyebrows. He wore glasses. Wire-rimmed, I think."

A picture flashed into Conner's mind. It had to be the same guy. He'd been front and center at the police station press conference.

Khemirra's nostrils flared slightly and she cast a quick glance toward the wooded area to their left. "That's all I can tell you," she said, this time pulling away and breaking the hold that Conner had on her arm. "I've got to run. I hope you find Patrick's killer." She backed several steps then turned and broke into a smooth, unhurried lope.

Instinct demanded that Conner chase after her. But reason urged him to hold off. His first duty was to the case.

Still, we watched her until she disappeared. He stayed long enough to ensure that no threat exited the woods and followed her.

Yeah. He'd help put this case to bed, after that he'd find out what had her looking over her shoulder. Then he'd pull her underneath him and feel her hot skin against his as he pounded in and out of her.

* * * * *

"Thanks for seeing me on such short notice, Professor Lisalli," Storm said, barely able to take her eyes off the set of gorgeous male buns that preceded her into a tight, cluttered office. The fact that several coeds waiting in chairs at the doorway also turned infatuated stares at Lisalli didn't escape Storm's notice. Damn! Maybe if there'd been professors like this when she was thinking about careers... Wow. The only thing better than the view from behind was the view from the front.

A throat being cleared forced Storm's eyes away from the bulge in the professor's jeans. "Call me Tristan," he said, eyes gleaming with something that might have been interest...or more likely, amusement at having caught her in the act of ogling him.

Shit. Storm felt the blood rush to her face. A couple of days hanging out with the Macho Squad and her hormones were going crazy.

She busied herself by opening the file folder containing Aislinn's designs and removing a paper that she'd created by photocopying and cutting so that it contained only script. Offering the page to Tristan, she said, "As I mentioned over the phone, this isn't part of an official police investigation. In the course of doing some background work, I came across this script and was hoping you'd be able to identify its origin."

Tristan took the paper from her and because she was focused so intently on his face—still having trouble believing that someone this gorgeous was a professor of ancient history, culture, and language—Storm saw the slight widening of his eyes before his gaze shifted away from Aislinn's script and back to her. "By background work, do you mean on a person of interest to the department?" he asked.

"I'm not at liberty to say."

His mouth quirked upward in a smile that had Storm's heart racing. Damn, he was sexy. Unfortunately, he knew it.

"I'll need to study this script a bit before I can comment on its origins," Tristan said. "I trust you have the originals elsewhere and this is my copy to keep."

Irritation rushed through Storm. He knew something but he wasn't telling. "Anything you can give me now would be appreciated, even if it's just a broad guess," she pushed.

Tristan smiled slightly. "I'm sure I'd be preaching to the choir if I told you that the more information that's available for solving a mystery, the faster the mystery gets solved. Right now I have only a page full of text that was probably cut and pasted from its original source by the look of it, but nothing else to go on."

Storm wanted to scream. She could spend weeks trying to hunt down someone else who might or might not be able to help her. Her gut told her that she didn't have weeks.

She studied the professor for a long moment before allowing her eyes to wander around his office while she tried to figure out what she could tell him. She was in uniform, which was in her favor. Detectives always wore street clothes, so there was no reason for him to connect her with the murder investigation.

Her eyes settled on his bookcase. Despite the general clutter in his office, his books seemed to be grouped by category. Greek and Roman Mythology. Inca and Aztec gods and religious ceremonies. Other cultures, some of which Storm recognized, most she didn't. They held zero interest for her. Vampires. Werewolves. Fairies. Elves.

Her heartbeat quickened and a smile threatened. Maybe she should sign up for one of his classes. She collected old books on fairies. She'd been known to spend a month's paycheck on an old, hand-illustrated children's book featuring the fey creatures.

Her love of that particular fantasy entity was the one secret she kept from everyone but Sophie. Not that she believed that fairies existed, but she wanted to, which was something Sophie understood, since she believed in all her crystals.

Sighing Storm turned back to Tristan. She'd never be able to pull off a complete lie, so she tried to stay close enough to the truth. She schooled her features into a dead serious cop look.

"I'm investigating a potential con artist. The text was found in this person's possession. Right now I'm trying to determine if this person is running a con, or whether they actually believe in—" her gaze flickered over to the professor's collection of books, "—in certain psychic phenomena."

Tristan's chuckle brought her attention back to his face. It wasn't the reaction she'd expected.

"Very politically correct of you," he said before his smile slipped away. "I take it that you're skeptical?"

Storm shrugged away her desire to explore the conversation further with him. Focus. She needed to focus on why she was here. "What can you tell me about the script?"

"It's Celtic in origin, ancient. I've seen something like it before. Offhand I'd say it's authentic. But I'd need to study it further in order to verify that and interpret what it says." He smiled slightly. "As you no doubt noticed, the script is elaborate and difficult. Though I'm no expert on the criminal mind, I'd think that most con artists wouldn't need to master something so complex in order to defraud their victims."

Some of the tension eased out of Storm's body. The scene at the station, with her telling the macho men that Aislinn was for real, had played itself over and over in her mind as she'd driven here. She'd dreaded having to go back to them and admit that she'd been taken in by a con.

"Thank you for your assistance, Professor."

"Tristan."

She smiled at his correction. "Tristan."

"I'd like to meet the author of this script," he said.

A momentary wave of panic washed over Storm. She temporized. "Maybe at some point in the future."

"Of course. The less attention that's drawn to this psychic, the better—at least until the Dean murderer has been caught."

Storm stiffened at his words and saw a flash of triumph in Tristan's eyes. Damn! How had he guessed?

As if he'd read her mind, he said, "I caught the news this morning. You photograph well." When she frowned, he added, "You were in an unmarked police car arriving at Dean's house. It was just a quick shot, but I've got a photographic memory."

"This has nothing to do with the Dean case," Storm lied.

Once again Tristan gave a small half-smile. "Of course." Then his expression grew serious. "As I said, the less attention drawn to the author of your script, the better, especially if the killer is serious about eliminating true talent."

A knock sounded, followed immediately by a coed opening the office door and peeking in. "Oh, sorry, I thought maybe you'd forgotten our appointment." Her flushed face was a dead giveaway that she had a crush on her professor.

Storm raised her eyebrows and said, "Thanks for your help. Again. I'll let you get back to your...academic duties."

With a wry expression Tristan said in a low murmur, "Leave the door open on your way out."

Storm turned and walked away, very aware of his gaze following her as she exited his office.

When she was gone, Tristan dropped the piece of paper into his office shredder and watched as it became confetti. Elvish. It had been a long time since he'd seen their script.

Motioning his student into the office, he sighed inwardly. The bad part of having faerie glamour was that it took so much damn effort to tone it down. And even then, some of it always spilled over when dealing with humans, especially the young and impressionable ones.

He grinned as he remembered how it felt to have the very attractive cop's heated focus turned his way. She'd sent his cock to full attention. Tristan smiled in anticipation. He couldn't afford to get mixed up in a high-profile case. No supernatural could. But after the Dean murder was solved... Well, then, she'd be fair game. His grin widened as he thought about his cousin Pierce. It had been a long time since they'd challenged each other with the seduction of a woman. This cop might just be the one who could settle his cousin's wild energy and keep him closer to home.

* * * * *

Captain Ellis stood at the window. Below everything looked normal, just everyday citizens coming and going, conducting their business without the presence of the media trucks.

Thank god.

Goddamn bloodhounds. They'd somehow gotten wind of the Morrisons' trip to the station and they'd descended like they were on a blood trail.

He rubbed his chest. The twinge in it wouldn't go away. It was going to get a lot worse before it got better. Either that, or he was about to have a heart attack.

This case was a nightmare. He'd be lucky if he didn't wake up in the hospital.

The intercom buzzed and his secretary's efficient voice said, "Captain, another missing child report was just called in."

"Details," he barked.

"Sketchy. But one of the detectives said it was a boy the same age as the Morrison child. He was at the mall playing video with his friends. He left early and by himself. When some of his friends came around looking for him, his mother called the police. There's no father in the picture — or so the mother claims. Says she hasn't seen or heard from the boy's biological dad since before her son was born. According to her, the boy and his stepfather get along fine."

"Shit. The news media have wind of this yet?"

A loud sigh at the other end of the phone was answer enough. "Sorry, Captain, the woman's already given a press conference, she says she's calling a psychic in."

"She say who?"

The long pause warned him that he wasn't going to like the answer. "No, sir. Apparently she told the news media that it would be too dangerous for the psychic — after what happened to Patrick Dean."

"Who's handling the missing person's case?"

"Bruner."

"I'll call and give him my condolences."

*   *   *   *   *

"I appreciate you being willing to talk to me, Madame Fontaine," Miguel said as he followed the well-padded older woman through a doorway covered with strings of beads.

Inside the room, dark tapestries covered the windows so that the only light came from pale candles in black lanterns set into the walls. Miguel had to choke back a laugh. Pure Hollywood. This was exactly what he'd expected a psychic's place to look like.

Taking a seat on one side of the table, the psychic motioned for him to take the opposite seat. "I invited you here because I sensed an openness in you."

Miguel fought to hide a grimace. It was a good thing that he was doing this solo. He'd never hear the end of it if Conner was with him, or worse yet, Trace or Dylan.

"What can you tell me about Patrick Dean?" he asked, wanting to avoid a discussion about how much of this stuff he believed. Aislinn's picking out the Morrison kid's glove had shaken him up more than he cared to analyze. Madame Fontaine's knowing smile made him more determined to ask his questions and get out of here.

"I will answer your question in a moment," she said before pulling a small velvet bag from somewhere in the folds of her dress and setting it on the table in front of him. "But first I must ask you to choose a rune from the bag."

The hairs on the back of Miguel's neck rose, accompanying a tingling sensation that had him wanting to look over his shoulder. "I'm on duty," he said, blurting out the first thing that came to mind.

The woman in front of him only chuckled. "Go ahead, choose one. I'm sure your captain would consider it a fair price for the information you seek."

Miguel's heartbeat rabbited around in his chest. It was one thing to watch this stuff, it was another to participate in it.

"I'm not so sure about that," he said. "The media would eat this up. They're having a field day right now." He could see the sidebar caption now — *Murder Detective on Dean Case Goes to Psychic for Reading.*

Madame Fontaine shrugged and reached for the bag. "I'm sorry you wasted your time coming here, Detective. I'm afraid there's nothing I can tell you."

Miguel gritted his teeth. Fuck, he was acting like a scared rookie. "Okay, I'll bite, I'll draw something out of the bag. But this stays in here. The department doesn't need any more bad press involving psychics right now."

Madame Fontaine studied him for a long moment before gently setting the bag down in front of him again. "Of course, Detective. There are answers you seek, let the runes help you."

Miguel closed his eyes briefly. Shit! He'd never live this down if anyone found out. Worse yet, he didn't want to get involved in this stuff, not that he was rabidly against it, like the other guys, but...

The obvious question would be about finding Dean's killer or locating the kid that just went missing. His gut clenched. He should be back at the station, not here doing this.

Miguel took a deep breath. He didn't want the psychic's opinion on whether or not they'd find the kid or the killer to affect how he did his job. Not that he'd let it, but why pollute his thinking?

Okay. A safe question. He could risk a safe question.

Storm.

Yeah, he could ask about her.

As if sensing his thoughts, Madame Fontaine said, "Concentrate on your question as you select a rune."

Do I have a chance with Storm?

Miguel reached in and selected a smooth flat stone. Removing it from the bag he placed it on the table and waited for the psychic to interpret the shiny black stone with its blood-red symbol.

Madame Fontaine picked up the rune and closed her eyes. "The one you ask about is not for you. Another waits in the darkness. You will meet her soon."

Miguel held back a grin. Okay. He could live with that answer. It was pretty generic. And he already knew he had to work on convincing Storm that he was right for her — no surprise there.

The psychic opened her eyes and placed the rune back in its velvet bag. "What else can I help you with?"

"I'm trying to get a feel for how Dean was viewed in the psychic community."

Madame Fontaine leaned back. "He had some talent if that's what you're asking."

"Did you know him?"

"I've met him."

"Can you think of any reason someone would have a grudge against him? Stolen clients maybe? Jealousy?"

Madame Fontaine chuckled. "Patrick was an intense man, somewhat of a loner. But he was a serious student of the occult. I don't think he was killed by another psychic. I believe he was killed by someone who hates all psychics."

Miguel's shoulders slumped. Yeah, that was a safe enough guess. This was another dead end. Hell, he could have done this by phone.

He couldn't think of anything to ask so he pulled out one of his cards and handed it to the psychic. "If you think of anything, please call."

Madame Fontaine took the card. "The news reports say that another psychic discovered the murder. Is she safe?"

"Yes," Miguel answered, wondering at the small twinge of uneasiness that gnawed at him even after he'd driven away.

* * * * *

Christ, could it get any worse?

Trace rubbed his hands over his face and stared down at his desk. He was so tired that everything was a blur. Between the Morrison kidnapping, the Dean murder, Aislinn, and now this second kidnapping, he'd gotten almost no sleep. Hard as it was for him to do, even he had to admit that he was useless right now, his head was so fuzzy that he could barely think.

"You'd better grab a cup of coffee before you head home," Dylan said and Trace jerked as though he'd actually dozed off.

Dylan shook his head. "Scratch that. I'll drive you."

Trace wanted to argue but before he could, Dylan held up a hand to silence him. "Don't bother. You try and drive and I'll have a squad car tailing you home. I'm sure the Captain would love to read about that in the papers tomorrow morning."

Trace grumbled something that sounded like asshole as he struggled to his feet. Dylan only grinned and said, "Hey, believe me, it's a small price to pay. It's great that one of us is getting some, and you were sure getting to be a cranky bastard before you met Aislinn."

At the mention of her name, Trace's cock stirred. But even it was too exhausted to want more than to just press against the warmth of her body.

"Let's go," Trace muttered and barely remembered climbing into Dylan's car.

Dylan worried as he drove. Despite his joking about Trace's reactivated sex life, it didn't sit well that Aislinn was so enmeshed in the case. Shit, in all the years that he and Trace had been partners, he'd never seen Trace so possessive and protective over a woman. Hell, Trace had always had a revolving door on his bedroom and more than once a woman coming through it had ended up in Dylan's bed.

Yeah, Trace could take care of himself, usually without even needing backup. But this time had Dylan sweating it. Things had a way of going bad when you got distracted on the job, when things got too personal, and this case already seemed way too personal.

"Man, we've gotta put this one to bed, quick," he muttered, feeling a knot tighten in his stomach as he stopped the car in front of Trace's house.

Before he'd even had a chance to turn the engine off, the front light came on and the door opened. His dick reacted to the sight of Aislinn. Damn, he couldn't blame Trace for fucking her. Even the spooky shit with the kid's glove wasn't enough to keep the blood out of his cock.

"Hey, Trace," he said, shaking his partner, "we're here and it looks like the little woman is waiting for you."

Trace shifted in his seat, taking a few seconds to orient himself. "Damn, I told her to stay in the house, out of sight."

Dylan laughed. "Better go set her straight then. Call if you need a lift tomorrow."

Trace grunted and climbed out of the car. "Yeah, thanks for the ride."

"Are you okay?" Aislinn asked as soon as he got close.

The concern on her face sent a jolt of pure warmth right through Trace's heart. Christ, he could get used to this—having her here at the end of a tough day. "Yeah, just beat."

She hugged him as he stepped inside then closed the door behind them. He didn't have the heart to ask her what the hell she thought she was doing coming out front where some reporter might get a shot at her.

"Straight to bed, or do you want a shower first?"

Trace's cock stirred, remembering the shower he'd taken with her earlier in the day. Maybe if he just closed his eyes for a few minutes he'd be able to...

Aislinn's laugh jolted him awake. Damn, he was asleep on his feet, literally.

When she slipped her arm through his, he allowed her to lead him to the bedroom and help him undress. The soft brush of her fingers and palms against his skin had enough blood flowing to his cock that he actually felt lightheaded.

"I'm not going to be much use in that department, baby," he said in a gravelly voice when he caught her looking at his partial erection. Her smile and the tender kiss she pressed into the center of his chest flooded him with feelings he didn't want to investigate or identify.

* * * * *

"I volunteered my services to the police when Thad Morrison was kidnapped," the woman being interviewed stated.

Captain Ellis reached for the bottle of Tums that his wife had put next to the glass of orange juice. Shit. The new reporter they had on *Channel 6* seemed to be making it his life's work to drag the department through the mud.

"What was their reaction?" the reporter asked.

The woman's face tightened, making her look more like a prune than she had moments before. "Condescending. They wouldn't give me the time of day."

"Madame Ava, have you volunteered to help with this latest kidnapping?"

"Yes, though I have to tell you, I'm nervous." Now the woman looked right into the camera. "My good friend, Patrick Dean, helped locate Thad Morrison. The police want us to think that the kidnapper murdered Patrick, but I don't believe that the kidnapper is responsible. More than once the police in this city have made accusations against myself and other psychics. Those allegations were thrown out in court."

The reporter moved closer to the psychic. "Are you saying that you think the police are responsible for Patrick Dean's murder?"

The woman's lips tightened. "I can't answer that question."

"Have you done a reading on the matter?"

"Yes, I have. But it's not something I'm free to talk about right now."

The camera panned back to the reporter and zoomed in for a close-up. "For *Channel 6 News*, your first choice for up-to-the-minute breaking news, this is David Colvin."

"Shit," the Captain muttered, shaking an extra Tums into his palm and picturing the mob of reporters that was going to descend, wanting details of any case where a psychic was hauled in. That assault was as sure to take place as the inevitable calls from both the mayor and the chief.

* * * * *

Aislinn sat in Trace's kitchen, painstakingly shaping a rough crystal into a work of art while Sophie drank a cup of coffee and scowled at the TV set. "What a load of crap!" Sophie said, hitting the remote control and killing the sound. "Where'd they find that guy—Tabloid-Sleaze-Is-Us? And what about that psychic? Please tell me she's not the real thing!"

Despite the seriousness of the matter, Aislinn couldn't contain a smile. Sophie's emotions always ran high when she watched TV. No matter what was on the screen, Sophie could be counted on to react to it.

"Well?" Sophie demanded, still scowling at the television set. "Is this Ava broad for real?"

Aislinn shrugged. "I don't know. Except for Patrick and Moki, I haven't spent much time around other...practitioners."

Sophie rolled her eyes. "Have you heard from Moki? Do you think she'll be mad that you had to shut down Inner Magick? Not that there's much action now. I didn't see a single reporter hanging out when I went by this morning. They're probably all stationed in front of Madame Ava's place, waiting to see if the police get her to help them find the kidnapped boy. Maybe you should hire a temp to man the store. In fact, if you want, I could probably take some time off and work for you." Staring at the creation Aislinn was making, Sophie added, "You could always pay me with a special design—maybe something that would enhance my love life."

Aislinn laughed. "Your love life doesn't need enhancement. Your phone already rings off the hook."

A flash of loneliness whispered across Sophie's features before being replaced by a grin. "That's my sex life, not my love life. Speaking of which, how's it going with Mr. Macho, also known as Detective Dilessio?"

Warmth flooded through Aislinn's body, coloring her cheeks and making her hands unsteady enough that she didn't dare try to continue with the delicate work she was doing. "That good, huh?" Sophie asked.

"He beguiles me," Aislinn admitted, glad for Sophie's presence and the chance to talk to someone about the feelings and desires that overwhelmed and sometimes confused her.

"Beguiles?" Sophie made a big show of lifting the remote control and turning off the already muted TV. "Tell me more!"

Additional color flooded to Aislinn's face. Always before it had been Sophie sharing her exploits and misadventures.

"Well?" Sophie prodded. "I need details. Tell me he's as good in bed as he looks."

Aislinn nodded. Her voice was almost a whisper when she added, "From the very first moment I felt as though..." Years of trying to keep the loneliness at bay made her hesitate before admitting her deepest longing, "I felt as though I belonged to him."

Sophie's eyebrows drew together. "Belonged as in 'walking down the aisle together' or as in 'I'm his possession and he can fuck me any way he wants to' — which is not a bad thought, by the way. The guy has alpha male oozing out of him."

Aislinn ducked her head and toyed with the crystal she'd been working on. "Both," she admitted starkly before shifting her focus back to Sophie.

"Oh, boy, you have it bad." Sophie tried to grin, but Aislinn could see the worry on her friend's face.

Sophie exhaled with a loud sigh. "Okay, maybe having it bad isn't such a terrible thing. He was totally possessive and protective about going to Patrick's place. I think it shocked the other cops. I know Storm was amazed. When she swung by last night with your drawings and your work supplies she said that as far as she can tell, Trace is acting way out of character. He's been a 'thanks for the fuck, don't let the door hit you on your way out kind of guy. And you're here, when the department could have just put you in a hotel and had some uniformed cop guard you. So my advice — lay back and enjoy it." Sophie wiggled her eyebrows. "Or stand up and enjoy it...or bend over..."

Aislinn laughed, interrupting Sophie before she could go through even more sexual positions. "Then you think there's hope?"

Sophie's smile faded slowly. "I don't want to see you get hurt. But on the other hand, if you don't risk your heart, then what you end up with is being lonely."

Reading between the lines, Aislinn reached over and took Sophie's hand in hers. Until this moment she hadn't realized how important finding someone to share her life with was to Sophie. She'd been fooled by how quick Sophie was to make a joke of her own broken heart and resume dating again. Perhaps this was the reason that she and Sophie had become such close friends. They'd recognized the loneliness in each other.

Aislinn's thoughts moved to the last conversation that she'd had with her mother. The Elf-lord, Rennie, had been there, his eyes crystal-clear in their arrogant disdain for anyone not of pure blood. He was her mother's heartmate now, had been for most of the years that Aislinn had lived in Elven-space.

Sometimes she wondered if perhaps her mother would have warmed up if it had remained just the two of them. If perhaps they would have become friends if not a true mother and daughter. Maybe if her mother hadn't been a highborn Elf it would have been different. But her mother was a princess among Elves. And while her mother's friends and family forgave her for exploring the human world and explained away her beguilement with the human because of his music, they never accepted the child she'd created and brought back with her.

Take care in your father's world, her mother said before pulling a ring from her finger and handing it to Aislinn. It was a heavy ring with small violet stones, masculine though finely crafted. Aislinn had a vague memory of seeing it on her mother's hand when they'd first come here to live. But she hadn't seen it in a long time.

This is your father's ring. He was a true heartmate or you would never have been conceived. But he was not Elven, no gifted as we are with the ability to touch others with our minds. This ring allowed him to join his mind to mine. I don't know if you will find a heartmate among the humans. But perhaps you will.

Aislinn had stroked the stones, finding a small measure of comfort in how they warmed under her hand. She'd kept the ring with her, but once in her father's world, the warmth of the stones had faded.

"I need to go to Inner Magick," Aislinn said as the picture of the necklace that she wanted to make for Sophie began forming in her mind.

"No way! Trace would make my life a living hell. He'd arrange it so every time I double-parked or went over the speed limit, there'd be some cop waiting to give me a ticket."

Aislinn laughed. "Only for a few minutes. You said that you didn't see any reporters there when you drove by."

"Right. But I didn't get out and check the bushes either."

"We'll be back before Trace even knows we're gone," Aislinn said, then defended her request further by adding, "I only promised to stay here yesterday. I didn't promise not to leave today."

Sophie snorted. "Somehow I doubt that Trace made that distinction. Just tell me what you need from the shop and I'll go get it. Better my face in the newspaper than yours."

Aislinn shook her head. When it came to creating charms for her mother's people, Aislinn's gift for working

ystal wasn't as great as even the least of the Elven
raftsmen. But when it came to crafting special amulets for
humans, Aislinn had a true gift, made more powerful by
her feel for creating at just the right point in time, when
the magic was willing to be harnessed.

Now that she had decided to make a heartmate
necklace for Sophie she couldn't let it go. She couldn't put
it off, not if she wanted to give Sophie a true charm that
would aid her in finding the one meant for her.

"It's important," Aislinn said, once again reaching for
Sophie's hand, this time giving it a gentle squeeze.

Sophie's expression wavered slightly. "Why don't we
call Trace or one of the other guys? I'd say Storm but I
think she's off interviewing some guy who wrote a book
about psychic investigations."

Aislinn shook her head. "This is something that can't
wait. It's not just going and getting the crystal. I need to do
some other things, to prepare. And you need to be there,
too."

"Me?"

Aislinn hesitated. She didn't want Sophie to be
disappointed if the magic couldn't be harnessed, but there
was no time to waste.

"I want to make a necklace for you. A heartmate
necklace. Among my mother's…people, there are
certain…clans who use a crystal to find their…husbands
and wives."

Sophie's brows drew together. "It doesn't make
someone feel something they wouldn't feel without the
necklace does it?"

Aislinn laughed softly. "No."

Sophie nibbled on her bottom lip before curiosity got the better of her. "How does it work?"

"If you mean how does the magic in the crystal work, then I don't know the answer. But the crystal will come to life and glow when you're around your perfect mate."

Sophie frowned. "And the catch is…I'm the only one of us that'll know we're perfect for each other. Right? The guy may have no interest at all."

"The crystal wouldn't lead you to someone who's wrong for you."

Mixed emotions flickered across Sophie's features. "So even if it never glows, at least I'll know from the start if a guy isn't Mr. Right?"

Aislinn nodded. "The magic demands that you give up something if you want to gain something."

Sophie let out a sigh. "I'll take you to Inner Magick."

Chapter Seven

ဆ

Dark, dangerous fantasies washed over Trace as he prowled around his house. Damn her! She'd promised!

He flicked his cell phone open, then closed it. Shit. He'd already left messages on Sophie's cell and home phones. He'd even tracked down Storm to see if she knew where her cousin and Aislinn were. Goddamn it! He thought it'd be enough to have a couple of patrol cars cruise by, just to make sure no reporters showed up. When he'd gotten the call that Sophie's car was parked in his driveway, he told them not to worry—she was authorized. That had backfired on him.

He stalked back down the hallway, this time stopping at the alarm panel. He should've changed the code.

Uneasiness washed through him as he studied the keys. They all looked the same to him. Even knowing which numbers he touched repeatedly, he couldn't see more wear on them than on the others.

Fuck. He saw the scene in the interrogation room all over again. She'd gone directly to the Morrison kid's glove. No hesitation. It was like none of the other gloves even existed for her. How had she done that?

Trace ran his fingers through his hair. He felt like he'd been thrown into a wall made of concrete.

He was too good a cop to start believing in this psychic shit now. But he was too much of a man to want to lose Aislinn over it. Christ, all he had to do was think about her and his cock got rock-hard. When she got home...

The cell phone in his pocket started ringing. Trace reached for it, pressing his already tight jeans even tighter in order to retrieve the phone. "Dilessio," he growled.

Sophie's voice answered him. "We're on our way to your house now."

"Let me talk to her."

"What? What? Sorry this connection is bad." The line went dead.

With a curse, Trace called her back and got voicemail. Son of a bitch. He didn't believe for a second that the connection was bad.

He stalked back to his bedroom and dug around in one of the drawers for a pair of padded restraints. When Aislinn got here she was going to learn once and for all that she belonged to him and he called the shots.

* * * * *

Aislinn shook her head. "I don't think hanging up on him was a good idea."

If Sophie was worried she didn't show it. "He wanted to talk to you. Yell is probably closer to the truth."

"I'm not afraid of him." Aislinn shivered despite the words. Some primitive part of her knew what was coming. She blushed as she remembered his husky warning in the shower, the dark promise it contained. *Don't come on my leg, baby. If you do, I'll punish you.*

Sophie slowed to a stop in front of Trace's house. The front door opened and Trace stood there, chest and feet bare, face dark and dangerous, hands on his hips—

bracketing the huge bulge pressed against his jeans. "Ohmygod," Sophie breathed.

Anticipation washed over Aislinn in a skin-tingling, electric wave. Her nipples tightened into painful buds. "I'll call you," she said as she eased out of Sophie's car.

Trace's body tightened with each of Aislinn's steps. He could read the need in her, the acceptance of what was to come. He couldn't have stopped it if he'd wanted to. It took all of his self-control to keep from pouncing on her as soon as she got close. He stepped back and let her pass, almost groaning when the scent of her arousal enfolded him as she moved into the house.

"You weren't supposed to leave. Now strip and let's get your punishment over with."

His cock tightened when he saw Aislinn's eyes flash at his demand. "I didn't promise not to leave today," she argued, "and besides, no one saw us."

"That doesn't matter. You knew I didn't want you to leave the house."

Her eyes dropped to the bulge in his pants and Trace had to grit his teeth to keep from groaning as his cock twitched under her gaze. He stalked her down the hall, using his body to maneuver her into the bedroom, forcing her backward until she came up against the bed. "You're under my protection. That means you do what I say. Now strip, baby, before you make me lose control."

Aislinn shivered, wanting to submit, wanting to please him. Her eyes flickered upward and met his. He needed this as much as she did.

"I didn't do anything wrong, and you don't have any right to punish me."

"Wrong answer, baby." He took her wrists in one hand and sat on the bed, pulling her down across his knees before yanking her dress up and exposing pale peach panties. His cock jerked in anticipation of where this was heading.

She began struggling, but he knew she was aroused by the telltale wetness of her panties. He ripped them down and gave her a sharp smack on one ass cheek. "Who makes the rules here?" he asked.

"Let me up," she answered and was rewarded by five sharp spanks.

"Wrong answer. Who makes the rules here?"

When she didn't answer right away, he escalated the spanking, sending fire across the globes of her buttocks and through her clit. Aislinn bit her lip to keep from whimpering.

Trace paused and ran his hand over her ass. "Ready to answer now? Who makes the rules here?"

His touch burned her sensitive skin, but Aislinn couldn't stop herself from moving into his hand. She was so swollen and wet, so achy with need that she wanted to spread her legs and feel him inside her.

"You do," she whispered.

He slipped his fingers between her legs and slid them back and forth along her slit before darting down to circle her clit. With the touch to her clit, Aislinn arched upward and sobbed.

"Right answer," Trace said, releasing her wrists and standing her on her feet. "Now strip like I told you to."

Aislinn pulled the dress up over her head and dropped it, never taking her eyes off of Trace. His face tightened and his eyelids dropped. She removed the bra and stepped out of her panties and sandals.

"Get on the bed," Trace ordered, standing and waiting for her to comply as he fought the need to simply push Aislinn down and fuck her.

Aislinn moved to the center of the bed. Her heart rate escalated when he didn't begin removing his clothes.

Blood roared through Trace at the sight of her naked and submissive in his bed. Christ, he wanted to rip his jeans off and fuck her right now, but he knew it wouldn't be enough, wouldn't satisfy him—not after the emotional roller-coaster ride he'd been on since he got home and found her gone.

He walked over to the nightstand, feeling her eyes on him, sensing her increasing anxiety as she wondered what he was doing. Anticipation rippled through him at her sharp intake of breath when he picked up the restraints.

He turned and attached the end of one restraint to the bedpost. "Lie down," he said, more aroused by this, by her willingly giving him control, than by the mock capture-and-fuck scenarios he'd played out with other women in the past.

Aislinn's gaze darted back and forth between the restraints and Trace. Her heart pounded in her chest, racing between fear and desire.

"Don't make me tell you again," Trace growled, his voice sending shocks of heat through her clit and buttocks at the implied threat of another spanking.

Aislinn shivered and lay down.

Trace fastened the first restraint to her wrist, then moved around the bed and bound her other wrist before removing his clothes and straddling her body.

He couldn't contain a groan as his balls settled on the smooth hot skin of her belly. His cock strained upward, demanding contact. Trace moved along Aislinn's body, his balls growing tighter and heavier with each new inch of skin they rubbed against. Her mouth drew him, but he got sidetracked at her breasts.

As soon as he cupped them in his hands, the need to push them together and ram his cock in and out of the valley between them seized him. Her pale pink nipples were tight with arousal and Trace had to give them tribute. He leaned down, sucking first one then the other, pulling the nipples hard and fast into his mouth as Aislinn writhed beneath him.

Each of her movements sent shards of pleasure through his testicles and up his spine, then back to his dick. Groaning, he pressed her breasts together and rammed his cock in and out of the tight hot channel he'd created.

Aislinn whimpered at the loss of his mouth on her nipples. She pulled against the restraints, willing to ease herself with her own hands if she had to. "Please," she begged.

Trace's fingers moved to her areolas and squeezed hard on the upstroke. Aislinn gasped and when the head of his penis emerged from between her breasts, she took it in her mouth and sucked. His body jerked in reaction, pressing his heavy sac tight against the underside of her breast.

She laved and sucked him at the end of each upward stroke until he was panting and nearly shaking with the need to come. She cried out and fought the restraints when he pulled away from her and rose to his hands and knees above her.

His hips gave an involuntary pump at the sight of her beneath him, at the way her eyes were dilated, her breathing labored, her legs spread, thighs and sheet wet from her arousal. Being outside her body was rapidly becoming more than he could stand. A fever raged through him that he didn't think would ever have a cure. He pressed his mouth to her cunt and thrust his tongue into her, drinking in her sweet woman's taste along with her cries of pleasure. When she tried to use her thighs to hold him to her, he pressed them to the bed and punished her by raising his head so that only his breath contacted her engorged clit and passion-swollen labia.

She whimpered and begged, tears streaming down her face as her need for him became unbearable.

He rose above her, a male animal in its prime, cock straining, testicles tight and full as the urge to rut became undeniable.

Trace paused long enough to release the restraints, and then he was on her, in her, demanding with every hard thrust that she yield everything to him.

Chapter Eight

❧

Nobody doubted that they were dealing with the same killer.

"Shit!" Miguel said.

"Yeah," Conner grunted, stretching and snapping a pair of latex gloves before pulling them onto his hands.

"Trace and Dylan on this one?" Miguel asked, snagging gloves from the box one of the crime scene guys had left next to the door.

"On their way."

Miguel shook his head. "Oh man, Trace is going to lose it if Aislinn knows this one, too."

They stepped into the psychic's parlor. She was stretched out on a cloth-lined table with a spread of tarot cards on her chest.

"Tell me about it," Conner said.

Miguel stopped next to him. "Oh shit. I saw this one on the news. Madame Ava. She wasn't a fan of the department."

"Yeah. I caught the interview. The Captain is hunting down Bruner right now to see if Sandra Kirby was using Ava to find her missing kid."

A movement at the doorway had them turning. "Welcome to the party," Conner said as Trace and Dylan walked in.

"A hundred reporters out there—any of them here when the murder took place?" Dylan asked.

Conner grunted. "Already got a couple of uniforms out there taking names and asking that same question. You recognize this one? She's been all over the news. Made a big point of not trusting the cops. Made it sound like we were harassing psychics and probably murdered Dean ourselves."

"Fuck," Trace muttered.

Dylan caught Miguel's worried expression before shooting Trace a look and asking the question that was on all of their minds. "Think there's a connection to Aislinn?"

Trace's entire body tightened. "I don't know."

"She's still at your place, right?" Miguel asked.

"Yeah." A flicker of uneasiness moved through Trace and he reached for his cell phone. Shit, would Aislinn even answer if he called his house? He could try and catch Sophie, tell her to forget about the beach, at least until he could be there to make sure it was safe.

Trace's gut twisted. He was a fucking coward. Sophie and Aislinn making a run to the beach had nothing to do with watching the sunset, but he hadn't asked why it was so important. Christ, he'd still been reeling from the sex. He hadn't wanted to open the box of psychic shit and have it all dump on him.

His eyes scanned the scene in front of him and he relaxed a little bit. It should be okay. As long as Aislinn stayed away from Inner Magick, she should be safe. This killer liked a stage for his crime.

He pulled up Sophie's number and called, half-expecting her to try and pull the static-bad-connection-bullshit as soon as she knew it was him. Instead she said,

"We just heard the news. Here's Aislinn. She said she didn't know Madame Ava."

Trace's heart did a little dance as soon as he heard Aislinn's butterfly-soft greeting. "You didn't know her?" he asked.

"No. I saw her on TV this morning. If she ever came to the shop, it was when I wasn't there."

"Good. You're on your way to the beach?"

"Yes."

Trace half-turned, trying to avoid seeing the smirks both Conner and Dylan were wearing. "Don't go near your apartment and the shop," he ordered, even though she'd promised earlier that she wouldn't go anywhere there might be reporters stationed.

"I'll stay away."

"All right. This is going to tie us up for a while. Don't wait up for me."

"Okay." Warmth seeped into every corner of Aislinn's heart at his casual acknowledgement that he wanted her to be in his home, in his bed at the end of the day.

"He order you to go back to his house?" Sophie asked as Aislinn handed the phone back.

"No."

Sophie let out a sigh. "I know it sounds terrible, but I'm glad it was this psychic and not somebody like Madame Fontaine." Chewing on her bottom lip, Sophie added, "You know her, right? She likes to use the runes. Her house is close to here."

Aislinn nodded. "Ilsa and Moki are friends."

"The way the reporters were talking, it sounds like Madame Ava was killed by the same guy who killed

Patrick. It sounds kind of weird, but do you think maybe the guy is kidnapping kids, then killing any psychic who tries to help the parents? Or do you think maybe it's just coincidence, and seeing the psychics get the credit and publicity for finding the kids somehow sets the killer off?"

Aislinn shook her head, unable to hold back a smile. Sophie missed her calling. She should be on the police force, or at least a private investigator. Crime and criminals fascinated her. "I don't know. What does Storm say?"

"Humph. Nothing. She hasn't called me back. She may still be out of town. Anyway, at least there's no connection between this psychic and you. That makes me feel a lot better. Finding out that the killer took the dragon crystals you made for Patrick really freaked me out," Sophie said as she pulled the car off to the side of the road near her favorite beach spot.

Aislinn got out immediately but Sophie lingered behind. Did she really want to do this? Did she really want to go through with this and accept the heartmate necklace that Aislinn had created for her? Aislinn would understand if she backed out. She wouldn't resent the fact that she'd spent hours creating the necklace for Sophie.

Sophie wiped her palms on her shorts and tried to calm her rapid heartbeat. She was curious about the necklace. She'd handled the crystal but Aislinn hadn't let her see the finished product. She couldn't even begin to imagine what it might look like. She shivered, remembering how the crystal had warmed in her hand to the point it almost burned. When she'd said as much to Aislinn, her friend had smiled and said, "It's responding to you. I hoped it would, but I wasn't sure."

"Maybe we should test it out on you first," Sophie joked. "You could make yourself a necklace and see if Trace is right for you. Then if he is, you could pass the crystal on to me."

Aislinn said, "When I left my mother's home, one of her servants gave me this crystal, but it never responded to me."

Thinking about it now, Sophie felt a small stab of pain for Aislinn. The few times Aislinn had mentioned her mother, there'd always been a sense of separateness, of rejection. Sophie's heart ached and she prayed that Trace wasn't going to hurt Aislinn. God knows, getting dumped was no fun. Sophie had plenty of firsthand experience at that. She got out of the car and walked down to where Aislinn stood.

"Ready?" Aislinn asked.

Sophie took a deep breath and let the sound and sight of the ocean fill her senses. Who was she kidding? Yeah. She was ready. Ready to stop getting her heart broken. Ready to find someone who could really love all of her, not just what they saw on the outside. "What do I have to do?"

"Walk out into the surf. When your mind is clear and open, dip the crystal into the ocean, then put it on."

"Shouldn't I visualize Mr. Perfect while I'm out there?" Sophie joked as Aislinn pulled a small cloth bag with strange symbols on it from her pocket.

"What's in your heart is already known." Aislinn handed the bag to Sophie. "When you're ready, take the necklace out. I'll go for a walk along the beach."

Sophie looked down at the bag. Was it her imagination, or did she feel the stone warming up? Her heart rate leaped. She'd been fascinated by all things magic since she was a kid, but until she'd wandered into Inner Magick and met Aislinn, she'd never really believed that she'd experience true magic. She'd never really believed that she'd actually possess something magical.

Nodding to herself, fully accepting what she was about to do, Sophie turned toward the ocean, only to jump at the sound of her cell phone. Damn! Thank god it had happened now. It'd be just her luck that some telemarketer would call at the moment she was dipping the necklace into the water.

Without looking at the phone, she pulled it off her belt and handed it to Aislinn with a small, nervous laugh. "It's probably Trace, checking to make sure you're where you're supposed to be."

Aislinn checked the number on the display and lifted the phone to answer it. Thinking she was right about the identity of the caller, Sophie turned and walked into the warm surf.

* * * * *

"Your publisher mentioned that you're just about finished with a second book," Storm said as she sat down on a tattered sofa and looked around at the dingy apartment. Obviously being a psychic investigator didn't pay very well.

"Yes. I am."

"Did you discover any true psychics?"

"A few had potential."

When he didn't expound on the comment, Storm forced air out of her lungs. This was going to be like pulling teeth. Damn. She'd imagined that the author of

Tales of a Psychic Investigator would be a hell of a lot more interesting than he was turning out to be. His book had been fascinating, which had surprised her. In fact, she was going to risk talking to the Captain about it. It would make a great manual for recognizing and trapping psychic con artists, since the majority of the cases Lucca had written about involved fakes.

She probably could have handled this over the telephone, but she'd listened to her gut, which insisted that she needed to talk to him in person. She'd been so sure that this lead would go somewhere.

Aislinn had said that Patrick handled Lucca's book before he was murdered, that he'd been excited. Storm grimaced and admitted that she'd let her imagination get carried away. She'd pictured herself dropping the macho murder squad egos down a couple of notches by making the bust based on Aislinn's psychic ability. As a result, she'd chewed up the day driving here and even told the Captain that she'd eat the cost of the trip. So she might as well make the most of it.

"Have you done any work involving psychics who could find missing people?" she asked.

"Some." Lucca leaned forward in what was probably his version of excitement. "Hard to verify of course. Most of the so-called psychics say they need to speak to family members or have them present. There's almost always some exchange of information and that increases the odds of the psychic picking up nuances and being 'right'. That and the fact that the psychic will usually provide a vague or generalized location, making it easy for someone to think the psychic was correct if the missing person is later found."

Storm relaxed somewhat. Apparently once Lucca got warmed up, he was willing to talk. "Have you ever encountered a situation where the psychic had no contact at all with the family, but was able to touch something and locate a missing person?"

Lucca frowned. "Yes, but it's rare. There was an old woman in West Virginia who seemed to have this ability. There was another in Texas. And a young woman in Montana. But there were limitations. In fact, all three had limitations."

"What kind of limitations?"

"The missing person had to be in distress and want to be found."

Storm's pulse did a little jump. Aislinn's talent was the same. "You didn't include them in your book. How come?"

Something flashed in Lucca's eyes. Irritation? Anger? Embarrassment? Storm couldn't be sure. She pressed him for an answer. "I'd think it'd be important for people to know that some of the psychics claiming to be able to find kidnapped or missing people are the real thing."

Lucca's back stiffened. "Unfortunately, these women never made claims that they had this ability, so I never challenged them directly. I learned about them incidentally, as I was investigating other psychics."

"But I thought you said that you believed they were the real deal. That was one of the things I loved about your book. It's obvious that you're part scientist, part detective, that you look for clues and evidence and don't accept just word-of-mouth testimonials," Storm said, hoping to coax him out of his defensiveness and get him to open up again.

"Yes. You're quite right. Exposing psychic frauds has been an obsession of mine since childhood." Lucca seemed to relax somewhat. "I took up residence near each of these women, then waited for someone to go missing. It's a strategy I've used before, though it doesn't always work. It depends on whether or not I'm able to make friends with the subject or with someone in the police department so that I have access when something goes wrong."

"How long did you have to wait?" Storm asked, fascinated and reappraising her opinion of D. L. Lucca.

"Altogether it took two and a half years, though I was able to leave on short 'business trips' and investigate other psychic phenomenon." His eyes sought a framed photograph that sat on top of a stuffed bookcase. His shoulders slumped marginally and he muttered more to himself than to Storm, "It took so much longer than I thought it would and after the first discovery I couldn't let it drop. I should have." Lucca's voice trailed off.

Storm studied the photo of the woman and child and read between the lines. Lucca's long absences had probably cost him his marriage. "I still don't understand why you didn't include them in your book."

Lucca seemed to roll in on himself just a little bit more. Defeated? Embarrassed? Storm couldn't tell. Lucca answered her question. "A newspaper reporter caught wind of the investigation and printed a piece about the first woman — the old woman in West Virginia. It got picked up by the Associated Press and reprinted. Overnight the psychic packed up her belongings and left town. There was absolutely no trace of where she'd gone.

"A similar thing happened with the second woman. And the third ..." his gaze once again flickered to the picture of the woman and child. "We became friends.

When she learned who I was and what I did, she begged me not to draw any attention to her. She said she'd be forced to leave if her face began appearing in the news." Lucca shrugged. "I was going through some turbulence in my personal life at the time and I let that influence me. I promised that I wouldn't include her in any of my articles or books."

Storm smiled in encouragement. "That was another thing I really liked about your work, that you were prepared to 'prove' your conclusions by posting your working notes on the website for your book."

Lucca's spirits appeared to lift with her complement and Storm felt herself softening further toward the intense man sitting in this neglected apartment. As much as she loved her job and wanted to be the best cop she could be, she didn't want to end up like him, alone.

Shaking off her momentary melancholy, Storm tried to concentrate on the reason she was here. Pieces of information swirled, their patterns not quite coming into focus. But rather than try to force the pattern into taking on a shape, she returned to asking questions. "When I spoke with you earlier, you said that you hadn't had any contact with Patrick Dean. I guess you've probably heard about the second murder, Madame Ava. Did you ever have any contact with her?"

"No." Lucca actually grimaced. "In my early days I studied and exposed so-called psychics like Madame Ava, but they're so obviously fake that I don't waste my time on them any longer."

"But you're sure you never had any contact with Dean?"

"Yes."

Storm paused for a moment before opening the large envelope she'd brought with her and pulling out the copy of Lucca's book that had been found in Dean's desk drawer. "Dean had this in his possession." She flipped the front cover open to expose the autograph on the title page. It was a simple signature with no note to personalize it.

Lucca didn't flinch or look uneasy by the revelation. He didn't race in with explanations or defenses, but waited for Storm to say something. She finally said, "Any thoughts on how Dean got this?"

"It could have been anywhere. The book has been out for several years. When it was first published I did a book tour and signed any number of books."

Storm hadn't really expected any great revelations, but she'd hoped, given how strongly Aislinn's claim had been that the book was important to Patrick. She pulled out a photograph that Sophie had given her and handed it to Lucca. When he stiffened she had to keep herself from pouncing. "You're positive that you don't know Dean?"

Lucca acted as though he couldn't take his eyes off of the picture. "Positive. Who's the woman?" There was a thread of excitement in his voice now, one that hadn't been there before. Storm's heart stilled for several beats. "Do you know her?"

"No. No." Lucca tore his gaze away from the photograph. "Those women we spoke about earlier, their features were similar to this woman's—delicate. And each of them wore elaborate earrings with crystals embedded in them, just like the woman in this picture."

It was Storm's turn to lean forward. "Were the women related?"

"I don't know. When I learned about the second woman, I tried to investigate her background but couldn't find any record of her parents. The same was true with the third woman, though she told me that her mother was deceased and her father remarried. I could never get her to say much about her father. I think there was some conflict with the new wife." Lucca pinned Storm with an intense stare. "The woman in this picture is psychic, isn't she?"

Storm was torn between her normal caution at sharing case information and her gut belief that Lucca might have important information that would help solve the case. "Yes, I think she is," Storm admitted. "Did the other women create charms and statues using crystal?"

"The third woman, the one I became friendly with, created something called heartmate necklaces." Lucca actually blushed as the words passed his lips. "I didn't investigate that aspect of her abilities. Crystals and the like have not been an interest of mine. It's too difficult to separate the power of suggestion and a person's belief in something with true psychic phenomenon."

"What about the other two women?"

"I wasn't able to get close to them. There was some indication that the older woman in West Virginia was a healer. The second one may have had an auxiliary 'power' for lack of a better word, but I don't have any knowledge of it."

When Lucca's gaze dropped back down to the photograph, Storm decided to take a risk. "I did a consultation with her since she knew Dean. She was the one who called attention to your book. She said that it was important to Patrick, that he was handling it before he died and he was excited about it."

Lucca's eyebrows drew together. "I'll check my notes and my records, but I don't know what the significance of my book would be. As I said, it's been out several years."

"Well, thank you for your time."

"You're more than welcome. Please call if you have any additional questions."

They rose and walked to the door. On a whim Storm asked, "The other women you mentioned, did any of them have family?"

"Only the older woman. She was married to a trucker. In fact that's how I stumbled upon her. I was visiting with the local sheriff when she called, frantic because her husband had gone off the road and was trapped in his truck. She was over an hour's drive from the scene, but she pinpointed it for the sheriff. He called for assistance and drove away — based just on that phone call — no evidence, nothing, he just took it at face value and left. I questioned his receptionist. She told me about the woman's ability to not only find missing people, but to know where her husband was. They'd been married at least fifty years. The receptionist claimed that they didn't even need to talk out loud any more, that what one of them knew, the other one knew. She said she'd talked to the old woman about it once and been told that it was common with 'her kind of folk' once they found their heartmate — that's what the old woman called her husband, her heartmate." He shook his head. "Unfortunately I wasn't able to verify the information firsthand. But without exception, everyone who had contact with either the husband or the wife, claimed that it was true — there was a psychic link between the two of them."

* * * * *

Aislinn looked at the number displayed on Sophie's cell phone with a mixture of dread and heart-pounding acceptance. She was glad that Sophie hadn't checked to see who was calling. If she had, then the opportunity to accept the heartmate necklace would have passed, and more importantly, Sophie would have been drawn deeper into whatever game Patrick's killer was playing.

As she watched Sophie step into the surf, Aislinn answered the phone. At the other end of the line there was only the briefest pause, then a slightly husky chuckle before Madame Fontaine said, "Child, I've been trying to find you. You're needed. This missing boy is in greater danger than the last one was."

Fear rippled through Aislinn, not just for herself and the kidnapped boy, but for Ilsa Fontaine. "I'll help, but only if you promise to leave town immediately," Aislinn bluffed, unable to bear the thought of having Ilsa murdered as Patrick had been.

"Yes, I'll leave."

"Do you have something that belongs to the child?"

"Not yet. The mother only just called. One of my clients gave her my name."

Aislinn's heartbeat tripled in her chest. "Don't let her come to your house."

"It will be all right, child. She's promised to come without the press or anyone else knowing that she sought my help. I haven't advertised my services in years, and with so many others courting the media and drawing attention to themselves…"

"Ilsa, it's too dangerous."

"She's already on her way. Can you come here, or should I bring the object to you?"

Aislinn's attention shifted to Sophie, noticing that her friend had moved farther away, but hadn't yet opened the pouch and brought the necklace out. There was safety in numbers, Aislinn knew. She didn't really believe that the killer would strike immediately. If she hurried, and her gift allowed, then she would be able to find the child and make sure Ilsa left immediately. Sophie might never miss her.

"I'm close to your home now," Aislinn said. "I'll walk over."

"Thank you, child."

Aislinn contemplated leaving a note for Sophie, but when she checked the car, she found only paper scraps and a dried-up ink pen. Torn between involving her friend and not wanting Sophie to worry, Aislinn decided to call Sophie's cell and leave a message, saying only that she'd be back to the car as soon as possible. That done, she dropped the phone onto the driver's seat and took off at a brisk pace toward Ilsa Fontaine's small beachfront house.

* * * * *

Conner's cell phone rang as they were finishing up at the crime scene. The Captain's direct number showed on the display. "Conner here."

"Looks like the perp is varying his style," the Captain said without preamble. "Bruner just got off the phone with the mother of the Kirby kid. She swears she didn't have any contact with the latest vic. Says Ava called her, but she never returned the call. Just an aside, Bruner got the impression Sandra Kirby might be in contact with another psychic, but for quote 'obvious reasons' he couldn't get jack out of her."

"He got anybody watching her?" Conner asked.

"Yeah, got a plainclothes on her and a patrol car."

"Good." Conner shot a look at Trace and breathed a sigh of relief. At least Aislinn was under wraps and not involved in this one. "Any chance of setting a trap?"

The Captain's bark of laughter was anything but amused. "Ran that by Bruner. He said 'no way in hell' was the mother steady enough. Just wants her son back and already half blames the cops for him going missing. If we get lucky, maybe whatever psychic she leads us to will be willing to help."

"Yeah, that'd be something. Anything on the kidnapping?"

"Somebody thinks they saw a van. So it may be the same perp who took the Morrison kid. We also got a match on a set of prints found at the house where the Morrison kid was being kept. Information's on your desk. Match is to some junkie with no violent priors—name's Maurice Houser—goes by the street name of Winky. Figure out what you want to do with it. Talk to who you need to talk to, and if you need some uniforms, you got it. The whole department is getting dragged through shit. For once you don't have to worry about stepping on anybody's toes. Even Bruner's almost willing to beg for help."

"Will do, Captain. We're about to head in."

* * * * *

"Child, thank you for coming so quickly," Madame Fontaine said as she wrapped Aislinn in a fierce hug.

Aislinn returned the embrace. "Please tell me that you've packed your bags and you'll leave as soon as we're done here."

Ilsa laughed softly. "Always the worrier. I'll leave as soon as I know the little boy is safe. Come now, the mother is already waiting."

"I don't want her to see me."

Madame Fontaine shook her head. "There's no time to hide your presence. The mother brought a worn comic book. I handled it only slightly and felt a terrible darkness when I tried to reach into the future. I was afraid to touch it further and destroy what you might need in order to find the child."

Aislinn felt as though a fist had plunged into her chest and wrapped around her heart, tightening its grip with each step toward Ilsa's darkened consultation room. She had no choice but to try and help the child, yet she knew that there would be no hiding what she'd done from Trace. Would he ever see that with her gift, she was able to help people, just as his skills as a policeman enabled him to do?

The painful squeeze of emotion didn't relent until Aislinn stepped into the consultation room and saw the parent of the missing child. Then there was no room for any thought but to try and find the boy.

"This is a friend of mine," Madame Ilsa informed the woman. "She's come to help." Her voice dropped to a whisper as she added, "Please remain very still and quiet."

Aislinn briefly took in the dark shadows and pinched face of the mother before her eyes were riveted to the comic book spread out on the table. Violent hues swirled from the pages, a hurricane of particles resonating with terror. Bracing herself, Aislinn reached out and took the opened comic book in her hands.

She was plunged into hot, stifling darkness, unable to sit up or move more than a few inches. The child's fear swamped her for a few seconds, and then her own fear increased as she heard the conversation taking place just inches above where the boy was being kept.

"Fucking kid saw my face when I brought him in here! I'm looking at three strikes if I get caught." The voice was a man's voice, but high-pitched, whiny…scared.

A hard-voiced woman answered, "You're looking at the death penalty if you kill him."

"Not if it looks like an accident. What if this building gets burned down? Maybe there's nothing left, and even if there is, what's to say the kid wasn't hiding out from his old lady, maybe playing with matches."

"And then we can kiss the money goodbye."

"What money!" the man shrieked. "Where's the guy who wanted this kid kept on ice?"

"Keep it together, okay? I'll go over to Winky's place and see if he's gotten a down payment yet. We get paid, then we can decide what to do with the kid."

"I don't like this," the man whined.

"You like opening your ass to anybody that wants to fuck it better? The money we'll get can buy a lot of inventory. There'll be enough goodies for you to use as much as you want with plenty left over to sell and keep the money coming in. Now let me worry about it. Here, this'll keep you busy while I'm gone."

There was the sound of footsteps, then scraping, like a chair had been pulled away from a table. The floor creaked as though a weight had settled above and to the left of the tight, dark space that was the boy's reality. Aislinn's heart ached for the child, for the terror he was experiencing, but her presence was outside of his awareness, and she couldn't offer him any comfort.

She concentrated on the boy's thoughts, on what he'd seen. What he'd heard.

Chapter Nine

ℬ

"Sure, I know who Maurice Houser, aka Winky, is. If his prints were at the house it's probably because some john took him there," the vice cop on the other end of the phone told Conner. "Too cheap to book a room. Or maybe the john was embarrassed that his trolling caught a bottom-feeder like Houser."

Conner sighed. It was a long shot, but what else did they have to go on? "Know where Winky hangs out?"

"Corner of Fifth and Davis. Flops sometimes in that abandoned building over on Thames. The blue one behind the old gas station."

"Thanks." Conner stood up and looked around. The only one in the bullpen was Trace. "I'm heading over to Thames, want to ride along?"

"The junkie?"

"Yeah."

Trace studied the rap sheet on his desk so he'd recognize Houser. Probably a waste of time, but sitting around rereading what little there was in the case files was making his gut churn. For the last half hour he felt like his skin was shrinking and the pressure was building. Twice he'd started to call and check on Aislinn, only to hang up before hitting the last digit of Sophie's cell number. Shit, he felt edgy, tense. Something had to break soon.

* * * * *

"He's still alive," Aislinn said, her soft voice sounding as though it was far away. "His wrists and ankles are bound with something, duct tape maybe. There's something over his mouth so he can't yell for help. It feels like he's in a compartment just below the floor. He's frightened because he saw one of his kidnappers. There's a man and a woman. They were just talking. The woman is leaving to see someone named Winky."

The connection faded briefly as the mother's sobs lessened the grip of Aislinn's vision. Ilsa's low whispering began to filter into her consciousness as she tried to calm the mother.

Slowly the woman's sobs grew quiet and the fear and grief swamping Aislinn subsided. The connection to the boy strengthened enough that she could be with him and know what he'd experienced.

"When he woke up, he was in the backseat of a car. There was a blanket over him. Its smell overwhelmed him and he was afraid that he'd vomit. He struggled to get it away from his face and the blindfold slipped around his neck. When the car stopped and the backdoor opened he saw a pockmarked man standing in front of a rundown wooden building."

Aislinn stilled the moment in her mind's eye, desperate to see something that would lead them to the child.

The vision blurred and faded for a moment, then sharpened. "He saw an address! One, zero, there's a hole where someone has broken the glass, then three, two, six, Griffon. It's printed on the glass above the front door."

Aislinn released the frozen scene and watched as the rest of it unfolded, as the pock-faced man recoiled in fear at having been seen, then quickly wrapped the child back up in the blanket and hauled him into the house, depositing him in the space beneath the floor before leaving for what seemed like ages to the boy. When the man returned, he paced back and forth, growing more agitated with each step. The boy's fear mounted with each footfall until the pounding in Aislinn's heart and ears drew her back to Ilsa's house, to Ilsa's frantic conversation with the police.

It took a few minutes for Aislinn to reorient herself, to separate herself from the vision. When she did, panic set in. The boy's mother was no longer sitting at the table.

"Ilsa! She's going to the house!"

Madame Fontaine put the phone down. Her hands were trembling as she began frantically searching through a desk drawer. "I don't think they believed me. But we can't let her go alone."

On unsteady legs Aislinn moved to the phone and dialed 911, insisting that she be put through to the homicide department. Whether it was the panic in her voice or the mention of Trace's name, the dispatcher forwarded the call. She almost cried when she got Trace's voicemail. It would be too late if she left a message.

Ilsa pressed a card in Aislinn's hand and she didn't stop to question how her friend had come by Miguel's card, she just dialed his direct line. When he answered, Aislinn almost wept.

"This is Aislinn, please, you've got to hurry. The missing child is in a rundown building. He's in a small dark space under the floor. The address is written on glass over the front door. One, zero, there's a hole where someone has broken the glass, then three, two, six, Griffon.

Please, Miguel, hurry. There's a man there and possibly a woman. The boy's mother is on her way there."

"Where are you?" Miguel asked.

"At a friend's house. I'll leave now. I'll be with Sophie in a few minutes."

"Get back to Trace's house!" Miguel ordered, then added in a softer voice. "I'm on my way to Griffon now."

Shaking, Aislinn put down the phone and hugged Ilsa. "We've done all that we can. They'll find the boy in time."

Ilsa returned the hug. "I've already packed a few things. My neighbor will give me a ride to the station. I'll stay with my nephew for a spell."

Aislinn stayed long enough to ensure that Ilsa's home was locked up and she was safely belted into her neighbor's car. "I don't feel right leaving you," Ilsa said, but there was no room in the small two-seater, and Aislinn didn't want Ilsa to be alone in her home for even a moment.

"It's just a short walk," Aislinn said, "and Sophie'll be there."

Reluctantly Ilsa nodded to her neighbor and he backed out of the driveway. Aislinn began walking along the beach frontage road, thinking to make better time on the hard surface rather than fighting for traction in the sand. She couldn't shake the feeling of anxiousness that assailed her. Twice she slowed, wondering if she should return to the house and take the comic book, but each time she resisted temptation. The less it was handled, the more powerful a tool it would be if she had to search for the child again.

There were still a few cars parked along the road and on the beach, their occupants lingering down near the surf or stretched out on towels. A van pulled over in front of Aislinn, straddling the line between hard surface and sand, as though its driver was contemplating whether or not he dared to drive on the beach.

Aislinn veered to go around the van just as the side door opened. There was only a second of awareness, an instant of seeing tanned arms extending from the dark interior and holding a small blue hand towel. Then the cloth was pressed to Aislinn's face and there was darkness.

* * * * *

Miguel didn't waste any time. He slowed just long enough to call Bruner, figuring the other cop had a right to be in on it.

"Thanks," Bruner said. "She lost the uniform, but my guy in plainclothes followed her to some psychic out by the beach. Saw some other broad show up, then the mother hightailed it out of there. Lost my man at an intersection. I'll radio him and tell him where we think she's heading."

"I'm on my way."

Dylan stood, checking his gun and reaching for his jacket as Miguel hung up the phone. "I'm with you," he said.

"You'd better call Trace," Miguel told him as they hurried out of the room. "Tell him to check on Aislinn." A bad feeling was starting to settle in Miguel's gut. He whipped his phone out and called Bruner again to find out which psychic the kid's mother had gone to, but the other cop was already moving and the call forwarded to voicemail. "Fuck."

* * * * *

"Damn this place stinks!" Conner said as he and Trace approached the rundown building. "Makes me think of when I was a beat cop."

Trace grunted in agreement. The smell of urine, garbage and stale bodies was just about to make him gag. "I'll take the back," he said, drawing his gun. He didn't expect trouble, but he wasn't fool enough to let the odds get stacked against him. Junkies weren't the only kind of people who hung out in buildings like this one.

From the other side of the building he heard Conner yell, "Police, Houser, we want to talk to you."

Trace stepped inside and listened for movement. When he didn't hear anything, he yelled, "Make this easy for yourself, Winky, come on out."

Still no movement.

Trace edged to the doorway and stepped into the hallway. Conner was peering into a room close to the front door. With the shake of his head, he stepped in Trace's direction. Trace moved forward, checking the room closest to him. The doors had been used for firewood or stolen, which simplified things.

"Place feels empty," Conner said, nodding toward a stairway.

Trace took a position to the side. "I'll cover you."

Conner took the stairs, moving quickly and silently for a man his size. As soon as he got to the top, Trace followed.

They moved down the hallway, choking as the stink seemed to get worse. When they hit the last room Conner shifted his gun back into its holster. "Fuck!"

Trace stepped forward and did the same. "Shit. Looks like Winky got into some bad stuff."

"Not very accommodating of him to kill himself before we could ask him what his prints were doing at the house where the Morrison kid was," Conner said.

"Goddamn convenient for someone that he can't tell us anything," Trace muttered as he walked over to where the junkie's body lay, a syringe on the floor next to it.

Conner pulled out his phone. "I'll call it in."

* * * * *

Storm knew something was breaking just by the level of energy she felt as soon as she walked into the police station. "What gives?" she asked the first cop she saw.

"Word's out that some psychic called in a location for the missing kid. Dispatch just got a call for a fire in the same building. There may be cops trapped in there."

"Who?"

"Don't know. Somebody said a couple of homicide cops were at the scene."

"Shit."

"Yeah, tell me about it. Probably got every reporter in town there as soon as they heard the kid might be there."

"Where's the fire?"

"Over on Griffon."

"Thanks." Storm hustled out of the building, more upset than she wanted to admit. The thought of any cop being trapped in a burning building—let alone a child being there—was horrible enough, but she'd gotten fond of the homicide cops, and it scared her to think one of them might not make it out of the flames alive.

* * * * *

Dylan's call came in as Conner was calling in the stiff. "What you got?" Trace answered as he squatted down to see if there was any evidence that Winky might have been killed by anything other than some bad dope.

"You want the good news first or the bad?" his partner answered.

"Well, considering I'm looking at Winky the Dead, better give me the good first."

"Winky's dead? That's convenient."

"Yeah, I thought so, too. Looks like an overdose, but him being a possible loose end and dead is a bit of a coincidence."

"I hate coincidences."

"Me too, partner. So what gives on your end?"

There was just enough of a silence for Trace to stand up and turn his back on Winky. He could already tell he wasn't going to like whatever Dylan was about to say.

"We got a lead on where the kidnapped kid might be. Miguel and I are on the way there, so is Bruner and at least one of his guys."

Trace's hand tightened on the phone. His heart started beating triple-time in his chest. "Aislinn?"

"Yeah. That's the bad news. Miguel got a call from her. Somehow the boy's mother hooked up with her."

"Where is she?"

"I don't know. Aislinn said the mother was on her way to where the kid might be."

"Where?"

Dylan gave him the address. Trace said, "Soon as we shake free, we'll head your way."

"Oh fuck, the building's on fire!" Dylan said. "Call it in!"

* * * * *

The scene was swarming with cops, firemen, and reporters by the time Trace and Conner got there. A hysterical woman was fighting to get loose from two cops twice her size. Trace recognized Sandra Kirby from the press conference she'd held when her kid went missing.

"Fuck. Half the building is on fire," Conner said. "You see Miguel or Dylan?"

They began pushing their way through a crowd of tragedy-thirsty observers. Trace's chest getting tighter with each step.

No Dylan. No Miguel. No Aislinn.

He was only a second away from going into the burning building himself.

Another fire engine rolled in, the men it carried jumping out and setting up hoses in a smooth, well-practiced synchronized movement.

"Goddamn," Conner said, not even bothering to hide his worry. When he would have surged forward, one of the firemen yelled, "Stand back," and Trace reflexively grabbed Conner's arm.

A loud crack vibrated through the air and a second later the front part of the building collapsed on itself, fire shooting upward and roaring in triumph. This time it was Conner who grabbed Trace as he lurched forward.

Firemen moved in with their hoses as black and gray smoke billowed through already broken windows and new openings.

Inside the house Miguel shifted Dylan's still form off a pressure point on his shoulder and moved into the last room. There was no time to stop and check to see how the other cop was doing, whether the blood from his head wound had slowed to an ooze or was still tracking over Dylan's face like a fast stream. Christ, just a couple of inches to the right and the beam that rushed past Dylan's skull would probably have crushed it rather than ripping skin and knocking him out.

Beads of sweat poured down Miguel's face and the back of his neck. The heat was blistering, so hot that the metal of his gun was burning its imprint into his skin. The heat he could stand, at least for a few more minutes. Thank God the smoke was taking an easier way out of the house. They'd all be dead by now if wasn't.

Last room. Last chance to find the kid.

Another wrenching crack sounded at the front of the house, followed by the roar of hungry fire. The floor shook, sending Miguel to his knees. Thick smoke rushed through the doorway just as Miguel noticed a sheet of plywood in one corner of the room.

He prayed as he crawled to it. Prayed that Aislinn was right, that the kid was under the plywood. Prayed that he could get it loose with desperation and bare hands. Prayed that there was time enough to get them all out of here.

Sliding Dylan onto the floor, Miguel reached for the edge of the plywood and began tugging.

Chapter Ten

જી

Trace's heart stopped for several seconds when the EMT guys suddenly grabbed their equipment and raced around the building. He and Conner followed, not caring when other firemen yelled for them to get back.

The sight that greeted their eyes was both a relief and a nightmare.

Flames were shooting from the first floor while smoke had begun to pour out of the second-story windows. Miguel was handing off a small child-sized bundle to a fireman in a bucket. As soon as it was done, he disappeared back into the building.

Trace looked around desperately for some sign of Aislinn or Dylan, his gut tightening when he didn't see them. The building began to creak ominously.

"It's getting ready to go!" one of the firemen yelled.

"Fuck, get out of there!" The fireman in the basket yelled toward the open window as he passed the child off to another fireman.

Another ominous crack ripped through the air. The fire truck holding the basket began to edge away in anticipation of the building collapsing.

Both Trace and Conner surged forward, unable to stand still and let Dylan and Miguel die in the blaze.

The firemen tried to buy a few more seconds by redirecting their hoses and shooting water into the area below the window where Miguel had been. Steam and smoke rose in an angry hiss of denial.

Miguel appeared again, this time with the heavy burden of Dylan slung over his shoulder. There was no time for a pass-off. The waiting fireman grabbed them both and pulled them into the basket just as the building heaved and shuddered. Seconds later the place where Miguel had been standing was a wall of flame and debris.

Storm got there in the final moments and began crying. It was embarrassing. It certainly didn't support her badass cop image, but she couldn't help herself. They were safe!

The EMT crew was busy working oxygen masks on the kid and the two cops even as they checked for other injuries. "How are they?" she asked, stopping next to Conner. Both he and Trace looked like they'd been to hell and back.

"Okay. They're going to be okay," Conner said as an emergency worker tried to get Miguel to move to a stretcher.

Miguel sucked in a deep breath of oxygen before lifting the mask. "Hey, I don't need a stretcher." He gave Storm a lopsided grin. "Don't want to be wheeled out like the old guy over there."

Dylan struggled for a second with the mask but Trace wouldn't let him take it off. "Better watch it. Dylan might owe you one, but it doesn't mean paybacks won't be a bitch if you insult him."

Miguel's laugh quickly became a cough. He put the oxygen mask back on before somebody else did it for him.

Two attendants hefted the stretcher Dylan was on. "Time to get you to the hospital, detective," one of them said. Storm frowned at the blood staining his face and soaking Dylan's clothing and hair.

"I'll be right behind you," Trace told his partner.

Dylan shook his head slightly, this time able to get the mask off his face before someone could stop him. "I'll be okay. Find Aislinn first." His voice was slurred, his movements disorganized.

Trace put the mask back over his partner's nose and mouth. His face was a study in conflict.

Conner said, "They're pretty sure it's just a concussion. His head is hard, he'll be okay. I'll stay with him. Got to monitor Miguel anyway. You go make sure Aislinn's safe." He looked toward the now flame-engulfed house. "We're going to have to talk to her about this anyway."

A muscle tightened in Trace's face, but he nodded and turned to catch the mother before she left the scene.

* * * * *

The warm touch of the heartmate necklace against her skin contrasted sharply with the cold dread in Sophie's chest. Where was Aislinn? Why wasn't she back by now? Why hadn't she called?

Getting more upset with each passing moment, Sophie once again replayed the message Aislinn had left. "She should be back by now," Sophie muttered as she checked the clock again. Between the time Aislinn had left the message and now, over two and a half hours had passed. Sophie had been out of the water, pacing back and forth for the last hour of it.

She was torn between calling Trace or driving along the beach and trying to spot Aislinn. She tried to think of reasons Aislinn might not be back and remembered the phone call that had come in just as she was about to take the necklace into the ocean.

Her heart did a small hopeful leap. She'd joked that it was probably Trace calling to check up on Aislinn. Maybe they'd had a fight and Aislinn was so upset that she'd just lost track of time.

"If he's hurt her, I'm going to find somebody who can put a curse on him and shrivel his dick!" Sophie raged in an effort to shore up her courage as she dialed Trace's cell phone number.

Trace's voice was curt and angry. "Is she with you?" he demanded, not even giving Sophie a chance to speak first.

"No."

"Fuck! Where are you?"

"On the beach."

"Close to where Fontaine lives?"

Sophie's grip tightened on her phone. "A couple of miles away. Why?"

"Get in your car and stay there. Lock the doors. Storm and I are heading that way."

Fear ripped through Sophie. "What's going on?"

"Just get in your car and lock the doors. Don't argue."

"What's this about?"

Only silence greeted her demand. "He hung up on me!" Sophie yelled and immediately called Storm's number.

"We're on our way, Sophie," her cousin said by way of greeting. Then with censure in her voice, she asked,

"Did you know Aislinn was going to meet with Sandra Kirby?"

"No! We came to the beach for something else. I picked this place! Not Aislinn."

"Well, she was at some psychic's place and now the kid's been recovered."

"Madame Fontaine lives near here. We were talking about her in the car, but Aislinn didn't say anything about going to her house." Sophie paused. "A phone call came in just as I was getting ready to uh...do what I came here to do. Aislinn answered it. I thought it was Trace. He's been calling my cell phone to check up on her."

Storm turned to Trace. "When's the last time you talked to Aislinn?"

"They were on their way to the beach."

"You hear that?" Storm asked Sophie.

"Yes."

"Would this Madame Fontaine know that Aislinn might be with you?"

"Sure. I guess. She and Aislinn's godmother, Moki, are good friends. And I've been to see Madame Fontaine a couple of times. But not for a while. Aislinn doesn't have a cell phone. If Madame Fontaine's been watching the news at all she would probably guess that Aislinn might be hiding out at my place. I swear, Storm, Aislinn didn't come here planning to go to Madame Fontaine's house. It must have been the phone call that came in because right after that Aislinn used my cell to leave a message saying she was going for a walk while I was out in the water."

"Well, her walk took her to the psychic's house. Not that Sandra Kirby would tell us anything. Dylan and Miguel went into a burning building to save her kid and she repays the department by total silence. Lucky for us, Bruner had a plainclothesman on her."

"Are they okay?"

"Yeah. But this is getting way more dangerous. The perp's all over the map. Do what Trace said, Soph. Get in the car and lock the doors. Anybody you don't know gets near you, drive away!"

"I'm already here. I can drive down the frontage road toward Madame Fontaine's place and look for Aislinn along the beach."

There was a brief hesitation before Storm said. "Could you find exactly where you parked again if you had to?"

"Sure. It's the same place I always park."

"Okay. Drive. But don't get out of your car. No matter what, don't leave your car."

"If I don't see Aislinn, I'll park down near Madame Fontaine's house."

"We're not far behind you."

Storm pulled her cell phone away from her ear and waited for Trace to blast her. She didn't have long to wait.

"I can't fucking believe you! I told your cousin to stay put!"

Storm gritted her teeth and counted to ten. And she'd thought that she was growing fond of the macho murder cops! "There's no way Sophie would have sat in her car and waited, especially if she turned on the news and got an earful about the kid being rescued. She's not stupid. She'd put two and two together and get the idea that Aislinn had probably walked to the psychic's house. At least this way we save time. And maybe we find Aislinn sooner. Sophie may be brave while she's driving around, but she's not going to race into Madame Fontaine's house. She'll lock her doors and wait." Storm crossed her fingers. *I hope.*

* * * * *

Sophie knew that she wasn't going to find Aislinn along the beach. She knew it, but she prayed that she was wrong.

It wasn't far to Madame Fontaine's house, not nearly far enough to account for the time that Aislinn had been gone. Aislinn walked fast. Sophie knew that from the power walks in the mall that she'd managed to convince Aislinn to take with her.

"Please let her be okay," Sophie whispered as Madame Fontaine's house came into sight.

Heart thundering in her chest, Sophie pulled to a stop in front of the house closest to Madame Fontaine's small, restored Victorian. She hated that she was too afraid to rush up to the house and check to see if Aislinn was there. But the closed door and darkened interior chilled her.

Picking up her cell phone, she dialed Storm. "How close are you?" she asked when her cousin answered.

"About a mile away. You there?"

"Yes. It doesn't look like there's anybody home."

"Stay put. Do not get out of your car."

Sophie shivered, near tears but trying to hold it together. "Okay."

A few minutes later Trace's unmarked car pulled into the psychic's driveway. A curtain edged back from the neighbor's window and an old man's face peered out.

Sophie got out of her car and called to Storm. "There's someone home next door. Maybe they saw something."

Storm and Trace held a hurried conversation then Trace jogged up to Madame Fontaine's front door while Storm hustled to the house Sophie had indicated. The front door opened and Storm flashed her badge. She spoke to the neighbor and then he disappeared. "Hang on, Trace," she yelled. "He's got a key. Says he took Madame Fontaine to the station a couple of hours ago. Aislinn was on foot, walking away from the house when they left."

The neighbor reappeared in the doorway and handed Storm a key. Sophie followed her back to the psychic's house, and despite Trace's frown, she went inside with them. If Sophie had any doubts that Trace cared about Aislinn, the rage and agony that she saw on his face in unguarded moments convinced her that she'd been wrong.

* * * * *

Fear ripped through Trace's guts. Christ, he should have ordered her back when the second murder was discovered. Or better yet, never let her leave after the Kirby kid was kidnapped and this whole bizarre scenario started to play out for a second time.

Bile rose in his throat. Yeah, and then the kid would be toast, maybe burned so badly that he'd never be identified.

Rage tightened Trace's body to the point that he felt like he was going to explode. He hated this psychic stuff. Hated it. If Aislinn wasn't involved in it then she'd be safe now instead of... He couldn't allow himself to go there.

He'd had years to see what people were capable of doing to each other.

Trace closed off the thoughts. Christ, he was a cop. He'd needed to think like a cop, act like a cop.

They'd have the techs come in, dust for prints and see if any matched with people who'd been at the other two psychics' places. It was a long shot and Trace didn't think they had very long. His gut told him that the killer was already working on his next murder scene.

* * * * *

Aislinn came to slowly, aware first of the stiff tape that sealed her eyes closed, then of the tape binding her wrists and ankles. The pain filtered in next. Her shoulders ached from being wrenched behind her back and bound to the chair she was sitting in. Her legs throbbed in time to the blood being pumped into them, but she couldn't ease the discomfort because they were also securely tethered to the chair.

"Ah, you're awake," a man's voice said. It was deep, rich, and seemed vaguely familiar to Aislinn.

Fear surged through her and for a second she gave in to the primal urge to struggle. The man only laughed.

"I'm sure you've got questions, but I'm afraid that I can't risk taking the tape off and letting you speak. Still, I find myself with some time, so I'll spend a few minutes and we'll pretend that you're conducting an interview." He laughed again. "I'll confess to being a little embarrassed that you caught me so unprepared. I'm not sure how long it will be before the proper tableau can be set up. Sandra Kirby played things a bit close to her substantial chest. As soon as she hit Oceanfront, I knew

she was probably heading for Madame Fontaine's plac
can't say that I was shocked when you showed up, thou
I had planned on you being the final act. But when th
good Madame took off, it didn't leave me any choice—not
with the police responding so quickly and the boy on the
verge of being discovered."

"You've been a surprise. I think you might be the real
thing, which has certainly kept me on my toes. Your friend
Patrick mentioned you when I called to set up the
appointment. Poor fool, he was so excited to think that the
great psychic investigator Lucca wanted to talk to him.
When I showed up and told him that Lucca had been
delayed, he didn't bat an eye. So much for psychic talent."

"Your friend talked about you, not by name, he was
too cagey for that, but he hinted that he'd invited someone
over who had amazing talent. Of course, I already knew
who you were. I was watching the night the Morrisons
went to see him. He didn't waste any time taking the boy's
glove to your little shop...what's the name of it? Ah yes,
Inner Magick." The man chuckled then went silent.

Into the silence came the sound of old springs
squeaking. Aislinn's seat shifted and she felt movement in
front of her. Her attention wavered from the man as she
took in what her other senses were telling her.

The air was warm, stuffy, smelling of cologne and oil
and vinyl. In a flash of memory, she pictured the van
pulling in front of her as she walked, the muscled arm
extending with its innocent-looking towel. Was she still in
the van? She strained for sounds that might help her
identify her location. There was nothing.

A latch cocked, then something heavy and metal slid
as though on runners. Stale, garage-flavored air rushed in

Aislinn knew that she was correct, she was still in the n.

"I'm afraid I must leave you now," the man said. "Time to do my part and report this latest development. Then I've got to prepare for the final act, at least in this city." The van lurched as he stepped out, closing the door behind him with a firm slam of metal on metal.

Aislinn strained to hear his footsteps, to hear anything, but the van's interior must have been padded with something that both contained and blocked sound. She fought the rising panic and forced her body to remain still, to conserve strength while she tried to find a way to escape.

Her heart threatened to deafen her with its pounding in her ears. Visions of Patrick's murder scene tried to press down on her, along with an imagined scene of Madame Ava and her tarot cards.

For a second Aislinn gave into the terror and struggled against her bindings. But the tape made it impossible to breathe through her mouth, to get air into her lungs fast enough. Shortness of breath finally stilled her.

When the burning in her lungs subsided and her heartbeat steadied, the skills that had helped her endure the taunts and isolation of Elven-space now helped her to distance herself from what was happening so that she could control the panic.

She wouldn't passively accept death. But there was solace in knowing that even if the killer succeeded, Trace would be spared the horror of seeing whatever tableau her murderer laid out. The Elders would never risk discovery by allowing a half-elf's body to remain among humans.

Aislinn began testing her bindings. There was enough give in them that she had some movement, but not enough for her to wriggle free.

She searched desperately for an edge to rub her bound wrists and ankles against, but the chair she'd been tethered to felt as though it had been bolted to the floor. It didn't budge regardless of her attempts to shift it closer to something that she might be able to use.

Tears fought to escape the duct tape.

The terror of dying threatened to overwhelm her.

Aislinn's heart and mind and soul screamed out to Trace.

Chapter Eleven

ଛଠ

Trace came to a halt next to the nightstand on Aislinn's side of the bed. Color from a crystal-embedded ring washed over the designs she'd been working on.

He picked up the ring, examining the delicate workmanship and strangely compelling beauty before tracing a finger over the elaborate script on her drawings. She was a mystery that he'd need a lifetime to learn.

His heart lurched at the thought that he might not get a lifetime with her. Christ, he should have told her to stay put.

She wouldn't have. Not anymore than he would have if he thought he could do something to find the missing boy.

Images of Dylan and Miguel in the flame-engulfed house flashed through Trace's mind. Without Aislinn, the kid would have been dead.

Trace rubbed his thumb over the small inset stones. They were the same color as her eyes.

If it were anyone but her, she'd be a suspect and not a victim. There were too many coincidences. Too many places where Aislinn intersected with the case.

But he'd stake his career on her being innocent.

He'd stake his heart on it.

The stones in the ring felt warm against his palm. Trace closed his hand into a fist and would have sworn that heat radiated from it, that by touching the stones he could feel Aislinn's presence.

Fuck. Now he was starting to buy into the psychic bullshit.

He set the ring down and turned. But the loss of contact with it left him feeling uneasy. Goddamn! He grabbed the ring and pressed it onto a finger then stalked to the kitchen before he had to examine what he'd done more closely.

Sophie and Storm were pulling plates and silverware out of the cabinets. Miguel was digging around for drinks. Dylan had defied doctor's orders and checked himself out of the hospital. He'd staked out one end of the kitchen table and was rubbing his forehead while Conner unloaded a bag of Chinese takeout, the smell filling the kitchen and making Trace's stomach growl. They were all running on empty.

"Everything quiet at Aislinn's place?" Trace asked, already knowing the answer but needing to hear it said out loud.

"Yeah," Miguel answered as he set an armful of sodas down. "I checked a minute ago. The Captain has three plainclothes on it. He's sending patrol cars by every hour and a half so whoever's got her might think he can outsmart us."

Trace nodded but didn't voice what they all were thinking. It was a long shot now that the killer had started to deviate from his script.

They sat down at the table and filled their plates. No one said anything until they'd eaten and the table was cleared of dishes only to be cluttered up again with folders and papers.

Trace shot a look at Sophie. The look she shot back said she wasn't leaving. He shrugged it off. They might as well let her stay — she was already in deep.

"Okay, anybody got anything new?" Miguel said into the silence. "The only thing I've pursued solo was a visit to Madame Fontaine." His gut twisted and he glanced at Trace. "No new leads there."

Dylan rubbed his head, fighting the effects of the concussion. Conner spoke up. "Trace and I tracked down Winky, aka Maurice Houser. His fingerprints were at the house where the Morrison kid was being held. Unfortunately, Winky is now conveniently dead."

Conner let the others process the information for a minute. "I talked to the Kirby boy and his mother. Not super helpful about the psychic, but the boy said he got a look at the guy who carried him into the house and put him in the space under the floor. There was a woman with him and they argued over money, then the woman went off to see Winky. The man freaked when she came back and said Winky had overdosed. The kid said it was the guy who set fire to the house."

"Shit," Trace said, getting up to pace around the kitchen. "Hired help. Dead end."

Conner shrugged. "Seems that way. The only other thing I have is the reporter. The Morrisons got the idea to visit Dean from her. She got the name from a reporter at the *Times*. I checked him out. He did an article on psychics about a year ago. That's when he interviewed Dean. Nothing suspicious there. Madame Ava wasn't mentioned."

"Fuck." Trace stopped in front of the window and looked out. He felt like he was getting ready to go through his skin.

Sophie said, "Was the reporter looking for a story? Is that why she told the Morrisons about Patrick?"

Dylan pulled his hands away from his temple and said, "She got one hell of a story if that was her motivation."

For a heartbeat there was silence. Miguel said, "Okay, here's a theory. You guys were convinced that the Morrison kidnapping stunk like a publicity stunt from the start. Maybe you were right, only the parents and the kid weren't in on it. The kid just happened to be convenient. What if this is really about dragging the department through the mud? We look bad because the psychics show us up, then the psychics get killed and people start whispering about police conspiracies." He turned to Conner, "Didn't you say there was a woman in the house where the Kirby kid was? Maybe it was the reporter."

Irritation flashed through Conner, a foreign protectiveness. "Khemirra isn't involved."

Eyebrows shot up around the table. Even Trace turned away from the window in order to look at Conner.

Through gritted teeth, Conner said, "She met up with some reporters and they started kicking around ideas on how to help get the kid back." He took a second to check his notes. "That asshole from *Channel 6* mentioned that his mother used to go to psychics. That's what got the ball rolling."

Storm spoke up for the first time. "I assume you're talking about David Colvin. He was hanging out over at Aislinn's place when I was checking things out. He's got to have a source in the department. It seems like he's always one step ahead of the other reporters."

The phone rang before anyone could say anything. Trace answered, listened intently, then dropped the receiver back in its cradle. "They've found a van a couple of blocks away from Inner Magick. The crime scene guys are already there. They've got traces of chloroform and a new baseball glove they think probably belonged to the Morrison kid. They've also got Aislinn's driver's license."

* * * * *

"Sorry for the cramped quarters," the man told Aislinn. "I hurried, but it was a little trickier than I expected. No matter though. The police have now found the van. I hated to part with it, but I needed something to keep them busy. And it does add an interesting little twist to the story. They'll find plenty of trace evidence, but no reason to connect it with anyone but the illustrious Winky, who is now dead."

He pulled Aislinn to a sitting position. "I'm afraid that I can't take you out of the trunk until we get to our destination. Just too risky. Don't fret though, we're not going far. If the air didn't run out while I was taking care of my last little errand, then you don't have anything to worry about."

Aislinn shivered when she felt his finger trace the butterfly earring. Where Trace's touch had been erotic, this touch filled her with dread.

"One of these will make a nice souvenir. I always take a little something to remind me that justice has been served." He twisted the earring and jerked, sending streaks of pain and blood down Aislinn's sensitive ear. She shivered again, feeling vulnerable, violated.

Once again the man ran his fingertip along her ear, only this time the flesh of his finger touched her skin. Repulsed, Aislinn tried to move away from the touch, but his hand followed her.

"Well, this is interesting," the man murmured. "I'll have to find someone in the morgue who can leak this out to the press. It'll make a titillating little sidebar." He traced the trail of blood down to where it hit the neckline of Aislinn's dress. She stilled as his finger worked under the edge of her clothing. Her heart thundered in alarm.

"No time for that," he murmured, almost to himself. "Maybe next time. Then again, that adds a layer of risk. It's an interesting thought though. Screw the psychics — literally." He chuckled. "Something of a poetic payback for all those times that psychics made my life a living hell. I'll have to keep it in mind. But not today. I'm afraid that my little diversion will only keep the police busy for so long. I would have preferred to set things up at Inner Magick, where you'd be in your natural setting. But your psychic friend has runes that will work as a prop, and since you sent her on her way after finding the boy, it's a compromise that I can live with." His hands slid along Aislinn's shoulders and forced her downward. A second later the trunk closed, drowning Aislinn in the smell of tire and carpet. She screamed silently for Trace, pleading with him to go to Madame Fontaine's house.

* * * * *

The ring on Trace's finger burned, drawing his attention away from the van. The edginess that he'd felt standing in front of his kitchen window had escalated.

Time was running out. He could feel it deep in his gut and the knowledge was suffocating him.

Fuck. He didn't care whether she was psychic or not. He just wanted her back. Safe. He wanted to come home at the end of the day and find her there. He wanted to make love to her, maybe even have a kid someday. He wanted her like he'd never wanted anything else in his life.

He moved away from where the techs were processing the van. Storm joined him. "Anything?" she asked.

"Nothing."

Her focus shifted to his hand. Trace gave the ring another twist and cursed inwardly. Wasn't he a picture? Standing here wringing his hands like a wimp.

Storm stared at the ring a minute longer before squaring her shoulders. He braced himself. She hesitated a second longer then said, "Look, hear me out before you start in on your 'I hate this psychic bullshit' rant. Okay? You're going to think what you're going to think, but I have to live with myself, too. Here's it in a nutshell. You remember the book that Aislinn said Patrick Dean handled before he died? Well, that's where I was, talking to the author. He's legit. In fact, Lucca's book would make a good textbook on exposing frauds. Nothing came out of the meeting that will help figure out who killed Dean, but something came out that might help find Aislinn." Trace stiffened and Storm paused.

"Lucca found three women who could locate missing people like Aislinn can. But here's the thing. When I showed him a picture of Aislinn, he just about came unglued. The other women had delicate features like she does and every one of them wore elaborate earrings with crystals embedded in them, just like the ones Aislinn does. Look Trace, I know this is going to sound crazy. Two of the women were single, but one was married. Lucca said that there was a strong psychic connection between the woman and her husband. When the husband got in a wreck, the wife knew and could tell where he was."

"You want me to buy into this psychic bullshit and try to 'connect' with her," Trace growled.

Storm stepped away from. "Hey, like I said, I know it sounds crazy. I'm just telling you what I found out. It's your choice what you do with it." She made a sweeping motion toward the van. "This might not even help us find her in time. What have you got to lose by trying it her way?" She turned and moved away.

"Christ, like I'd even know what to do," Trace muttered, rubbing his hands over his face and feeling the burn of the ring against his skin.

He closed his eyes, not really meaning to accept Storm's suggestion, and yet desperate enough to try it. It was easy enough to concentrate on the ring's heat, on the way it seemed to radiate from his finger to his face, slowly expanding until it touched his heart. *Where are you?* he screamed silently, wanting an answer and yet afraid of confronting a dark void and facing the possibility that she might already be dead.

The ring flared against his skin, making his heart jump. The smell of the ocean flooded his nostril along with the image of Madame Fontaine's house.

Trace didn't stop to question what was happening to him, he spun around and headed for the car, stopping only long enough to grab Conner. "I think he's going to take her back to Madame Fontaine's house. That's where he's going to stage it. Tell Dylan to stay here and cover this. Grab Miguel," he hesitated, "and Storm."

Chapter Twelve

The car eased to a stop. Even locked in the trunk, Aislinn could feel the power of the ocean. Had she really touched Trace's mind? Or did she simply want to believe that he would find her in time, and that she wasn't going to die?

A car door opened and closed, then the trunk lifted and fresh ocean air rushed in. "We're here," the man said, his voice higher now, full of anticipation. "I'm afraid I can't linger. Things have gotten a little hotter. But more interesting—much, much more interesting." He clucked. "The police radio is burning up with chatter tonight, it's delicious really. A murder cop with a psychic girlfriend. How do you think we should slant it? What about— *Furious cop boyfriend tries to cover up homicide by staging copycat murder*? It has a certain pizzazz to it."

Aislinn was lifted from the trunk. "Good thing your psychic friend has a private entrance for clients afraid of being seen here."

She struggled, unwilling to allow him to carry her into the house without putting up a fight. He tightened his grip until pain and lack of breath forced her to stop. She reached for Trace, sending her terror and her desperation.

* * * * *

Anguish flooded through Trace. "Christ, we're not going to make it in time," he said, taking a curve fast and sending Conner slamming into the passenger door.

The police radio chirped to life, giving feedback on what units were nearing the psychic's house. Trace took another turn then slammed the gas pedal down when he hit the beach frontage road.

Conner picked up the radio and signaled their position. In the rearview mirror he could see the car Miguel and Storm were in. Miguel's voice crackled over the radio, "There's a private entrance on the opposite side of the house—left side if you're facing the ocean. If the perp's here, he may have his car parked out of sight there."

"We'll take that entrance," Trace said and Conner repeated it into the radio.

"Acknowledged," Miguel replied.

* * * * *

Aislinn's struggles slowed the man, but didn't stop him. The smell of Ilsa's aromatic candles grew stronger as his footsteps echoed in the quiet of the house.

He used Aislinn's arm and shoulder to push through the door to the consultation room. In her mind's eye, she could see the room perfectly.

The click of his lighter sounded sharp and grew more unnerving as he made his way around the room, lighting candles. When the last one was lit, he laid her on the cloth-covered table.

Aislinn heard the rustle of material and the soft brush of stone against stone. "It would have been more appropriate to use these with Madame Fontaine, but necessity dictates, I'm afraid." There was more rustling, then Aislinn felt Ilsa's runes drop onto her chest. "My mother was a fan of all things psychic. She squandered every dime she had and listened to every crackpot who hung a shingle out. If it had just been her life, then I could be a little more forgiving about it, but I'm afraid she had the tendency to use her psychics as a source for child-rearing. Most took the easy way out, of course, telling her things like, 'I see good things in store for your son', which meant my mother left me to my own devices and didn't interfere. But some of them took special delight in dire predictions. After a while, I grew to hate them." He gave a slightly embarrassed laugh.

"Sorry to ramble, but until now there's been only a limited amount of conversation. Your showing up early at Patrick's home just about gave me a heart attack. I had to act quickly. Madame Ava was such an irritating person that I couldn't envision myself spending a second longer than necessary with her. Horrid. The forced interaction whenever she got in front of the cameras was bad enough, even if it did add to the story immeasurably."

The cold edge of a blade pressed against Aislinn's neck. She stiffened and tried to move away.

"Stay still or you'll accidentally cut yourself." The blade traveled upward, across her cheek, then stilled near her eyes. "I'm afraid that I can't do anything about your other bindings until after we're finished, but it's only fair that we meet face-to-face."

The blade sliced through the duct tape, opening a small cut as it did, but the blood oozed instead of running down the side of Aislinn's face. "This is going to hurt," he said as he ripped the duct tape covering her eyes away.

Aislinn's body arched in reaction, her scream trapped in her throat, though her lips burned as they tried to open against the tape. Tears streamed out of her eyes, stinging her face as they rolled over the knife cut.

"Surprised?" he asked, then tensed, head jerking upward at the sound of splintering wood.

As heavy footsteps pounded down the hallway of the small house, the reporter Aislinn had seen on TV grabbed her still bound body and pulled it against the front of his as Trace barreled in, gun drawn, murder on his face.

The knife at Aislinn's throat cut into skin and sent a flow of blood down the front of her neck. "Don't come any closer," her kidnapper said.

Rage and joy collided in Trace's chest.

She was alive.

He sensed Conner hovering just inside the private entrance. Miguel was at the other end of the hall. Trace held up his hand to halt him. "David Colvin, *Channel 6*, right? Get tired of reporting news and decide to make it instead?"

"Very good, Detective Dilessio."

Trace heartbeat kicked up. So the guy knew who he was. "Might as well put the knife down, end this before someone gets hurt."

"I imagine it's alarming to see a knife held so close to your girlfriend's very pretty throat."

Trace broke eye contact with the reporter just long enough to look at Aislinn's face. He expected to see terror, but instead felt the warm rush of her confidence in him.

"Let's end this now, Colvin."

The knife seemed to dig a little deeper in Aislinn's neck. Trace tried not to react.

"Please, this script is so unoriginal," the reporter said. His knuckles glowed white against the black handle of the knife. Reflected light from the candles flickered against the blade.

"What do you want?" Trace asked.

"Let's start with your gun, so I'll have a fighting chance of getting out of here alive."

Trace's gut twisted. Rule number one—never give up your gun. Would she understand that he couldn't do that? Couldn't put even more lives in jeopardy?

I understand.

His eyes flashed to hers. Had he imagined her voice?

I understand, her voice whispered again through his mind before she stiffened and her face tightened with pain.

"You're stalling. Give me your gun."

Trace's entire body surged with rage as he saw that the wound on her neck was deeper now, the blood flowing more freely. "How do I know you won't kill her anyway?"

"You don't. But I promise that I will kill her if it looks like I'm going to be arrested. Not much to lose at that point."

There was no room for a headshot, no hope that a sniper could take Colvin out since there were no visible windows in the room. If only…

I can distract him. I can make him take all of my weight.

In desperation, Trace answered, *Christ, I don't even know if your voice is real or if I'm imagining it!*

He took my earring as a souvenir.

217

The thought startled Trace. His attention swung to the knife, the slender column of her neck, higher. He could see the delicate wing of one butterfly earring, but the other was covered by hair.

Had his subconscious noticed a missing earring?

Ask him.

This time the voice seemed stronger, more real in his mind.

Trace shifted the gun back and forth between his hands, as though he was considering giving it up. "I want her safe. I want all of her back. No souvenirs."

Colvin's eyes widened in surprise, then he chuckled. "Not quite out of the closet, so to speak. You don't want your police friends to see how different she really is. The ears are a nice touch. If it's any consolation, I think she might be the real thing." His features reformed, this time with a trace of panic as police sirens wailed and echoed, growing closer. "Time to write the headline. What's it going to be? *Cops trade killer for psychic* or *Homicide detective watches psychic girlfriend's death as killer is finally stopped.*"

Trace steadied the gun and himself. *Ready?*

He watched her eyes. *Yes.*

Now!

She sagged, and for a split second Colvin's head was exposed.

Trace took the shot.

Chapter Thirteen

ഔ

Despite the heat radiating off of Trace's body, Aislinn shivered as he carried her through the door leading from the garage into his house. It seemed like a lifetime had passed since she and Sophie left for the beach.

"How's the throat?" Trace asked, hugging her more tightly to his body.

"It'll heal."

"You should have let the EMT guys look at it."

"I couldn't." She felt him tense against her but he didn't speak again until he'd carried her to the bathroom and set her gently on the countertop. Cupping her face in hands that still smelled of gunpowder, Trace asked, "What did he mean when he said that the ears were a nice touch?"

Aislinn searched his face. "They're different. They're part of my heritage."

"Like being able to find missing people?"

"Only some of them."

Trace closed his eyes briefly, daring himself to face the truth. *What about this? How can we hear each other like this?*

Aislinn reached over and touched the ring on Trace's finger. *My mother was psychic, but my father wasn't. When they formed a bond, she gave this ring to him so they could communicate in the way of her people.*

"It's a wedding band?"

219

Was that panic in his voice? "There was never a formal marriage ceremony."

Trace pushed her hair away from first one ear, then the other, exposing the delicate crystal-lined butterflies perched at the top. He'd thought she'd mentioned the stolen earring as a way of getting him to accept their unspoken communication, but despite what she'd endured, she'd been frantic about retrieving the earring and putting it back on.

"Show me," he whispered, husky demand and plea bundled together as he ran his finger over each intricately crafted butterfly wing.

For several long seconds Aislinn searched his face. Finally she removed the earrings and exposed delicate pointed tips.

Trace stroked the smooth skin. "Natural?" he asked, already knowing the answer.

"Yes. All of my mother's people have ears like this."

"Elf-like."

Aislinn stilled.

Trace tensed then gave a slightly shaky laugh. "Don't tell me. I think I've had to deal with enough psychic shit for today." He pressed his body to hers and wrapped her in his arms. "We're going to have to agree on some rules, some limits. I can't go through this again. When I knew you were missing and he probably had you, I..." He tightened his grip. "I didn't care whether you were psychic or not. I just wanted you back. Safe. All I could think about was how I needed you in my life, how I wanted you to be waiting for me at the end of the day. Christ, Aislinn, I want you like I've never wanted anything in my life." He pulled back so he could read her face.

Aislinn leaned forward and brushed her lips against his. "I want you the same way." She hesitated before adding, "You're my heartmate. Among my mother's people, it's a lifelong commitment."

"Good. Because it's probably going to take me a lifetime to come to terms with the psychic sh…"

Aislinn stopped him with the press of her mouth on his. *Until you beguiled me, I kept the hope of having a heartmate locked inside. I need you. I need to feel your strength. Your love. I need to belong to you…to be claimed…possessed.* The last word was a faint whisper in Trace's mind but it sent lava-hot blood roaring to his cock.

He moved back and started removing his clothes. Aislinn's fingers went to the buttons at the front of her dress and Trace's eyelids lowered, his face hardened. *That's right, baby, strip. As soon as we get you cleaned up, I'm going to run my hands and mouth over every inch of you. Then I'm going to show you with my cock just how much you belong to me. And when I'm done, there won't be any doubt in your mind that I love you.*

Why an electronic book?

We live in the Information Age—an exciting time in the history of human civilization, in which technology rules supreme and continues to progress in leaps and bounds every minute of every day. For a multitude of reasons, more and more avid literary fans are opting to purchase e-books instead of paper books. The question from those not yet initiated into the world of electronic reading is simply: *Why?*

1. *Price.* An electronic title at Ellora's Cave Publishing and Cerridwen Press runs anywhere from 40% to 75% less than the cover price of the exact same title in paperback format. Why? Basic mathematics and cost. It is less expensive to publish an e-book (no paper and printing, no warehousing and shipping) than it is to publish a paperback, so the savings are passed along to the consumer.

2. *Space.* Running out of room in your house for your books? That is one worry you will never have with electronic books. For a low one-time cost, you can purchase a handheld device specifically designed for e-reading. Many e-readers have large, convenient screens for viewing. Better yet, hundreds of titles can be stored within your new library—on a single microchip. There a variety of e-readers from different manufacturers. You can also read e-books on your PC or laptop computer. (Please note that Ellora's

Cave does not endorse any specific brands. You can check our websites at www.ellorascave.com or www.cerridwenpress.com for information we make available to new consumers.)

3. *Mobility.* Because your new e-library consists of only a microchip within a small, easily transportable e-reader, your entire cache of books can be taken with you wherever you go.

4. ***Personal Viewing Preferences.*** Are the words you are currently reading too small? Too large? Too... ANNOYING? Paperback books cannot be modified according to personal preferences, but e-books can.

5. ***Instant Gratification.*** Is it the middle of the night and all the bookstores near you are closed? Are you tired of waiting days, sometimes weeks, for bookstores to ship the novels you bought? Ellora's Cave Publishing sells instantaneous downloads twenty-four hours a day, seven days a week, every day of the year. Our webstore is never closed. Our e-book delivery system is 100% automated, meaning your order is filled as soon as you pay for it.

Those are a few of the top reasons why electronic books are replacing paperbacks for many avid readers.

As always, Ellora's Cave and Cerridwen Press welcome your questions and comments. We invite you to email us at Comments@ellorascave.com or write to us directly at Ellora's Cave Publishing Inc., 1056 Home Avenue, Akron, OH 44310-3502.

Discover for yourself why readers can't get enough of the multiple award-winning publisher

Ellora's Cave.

Whether you prefer e-books or paperbacks,

be sure to visit EC on the web at www.ellorascave.com

for an erotic reading experience that will leave you breathless.